Portraits of Forgiveness

To my friend and fellow education lawyer Deborah — Thanks for all your help and best wishes always —
Pat Pauw
04.05.02

PORTRAITS OF FORGIVENESS
▼

E. Patrick Hull

Writers Club Press
San Jose New York Lincoln Shanghai

Portraits of Forgiveness

All Rights Reserved © 2001 by Erwin Patrick Hull

No part of this book may be reproduced or transmitted in any form or by any means, graphic, electronic, or mechanical, including photocopying, recording, taping, or by any information storage retrieval system, without the permission in writing from the publisher.

Writers Club Press
an imprint of iUniverse.com, Inc.

For information address:
iUniverse.com, Inc.
5220 S 16th, Ste. 200
Lincoln, NE 68512
www.iuniverse.com

ISBN: 0-595-17801-4

Printed in the United States of America

To the people of the great state of Tennessee. Special thanks to my three sons, Daniel, Christopher and Michael who are the greatest, and to the following who have shaped my thoughts in writing this book: Perry Lynn, Raymond, all the great folks at the Tennessee School for the Deaf, Linda Jane, Phyllis, Jack, Martha, Calvin, Vickie C., the good people of Marion County, and finally to Phil Carter who read one of the early drafts of my book and liked it (which, in itself, was encouraging, but not necessarily a good omen). Also, thanks to Judge Richard E. Ladd of Bristol, Tennessee for the Horace Stoneham joke, told to me one day while we were waiting for a jury to come back.

Preface

This is a tale of life, love and the law in rural Tennessee. I have tried to be true to the ups and downs, joys and struggles of all three. Each character is fictitious and many are a composite of some of the clients, friends, lawyers and characters I have encountered along the way. Likewise, the case is totally fictitious-a composite of research, conversations and imagination. Marion County and Jasper are real, and I am thankful for the opportunity to have tried a case there several years ago.

Part I

"…and forgive us our trespasses as we forgive those who trespass against us."

The Lord's Prayer

CHAPTER 1

▼

Anne sat at her desk and waited. She was trying to look busy, but her heart wasn't in it. She glanced at her watch. 3:15. The little gears and wheels which had been grinding all day in her stomach shifted into a higher gear. It was time.

She closed the file which had been resting in her lap and laid it on the corner of her desk, picked up her purse and started out. Her path to the front door took her by the receptionist's desk.

"I guess I'm outta here—be back on Monday." She walked to the dirty old pegboard and moved the peg across from her name into the "Out" column. The receptionist gave her a motherly look.

"You have a good time and be careful."

"Don't worry, I will."

A voice boomed from the rear of the office. "Why are you always the one that gets to go to the good meetings?"

"Don't know—Gotta go." Anne rolled her eyes and slipped out the front door.

"Why does she always get to go? The Department has two of these meetings a year, and she always gets to go to the one at the Opryland. Something ain't right somewhere."

"Oh, ease up a little, she deserves all the time off she can get."

"You saying I don't?"

"I'd say she deserves it more after all she's been through. I never saw anybody that tense in all my life."

Anne walked outside, shook her head and flipped her long red hair over her shoulder. Mentally, she shook the thoughts of the office out of her mind. Her eyes, surrounded by freckles, always seemed to be squinting, and they were narrowed in concentration today.

Chill bumps crept up her arms. The little hairs on her arms stood on end. She was wearing a light cotton blouse—too cool for the day—and khaki slacks. She crossed her arms around her waist and jogged on her toes to her car. Once inside, she sat and stared into the distance.

She had been in a far-off mood all day. It was as if she was another person and could watch herself going about her activities. Her mind was focused on the task that lay ahead, and everything else was blurred like the fuzzy foreground of a distantly focused photograph. Now it was time to get down to business.

She started the car, turned off the radio and pulled out of the parking lot. Her mind was ticking off the steps to a plan she had been formulating for nearly a year. It had taken most of that time to find the right opportunity, and she didn't intend to mess things up now.

She rummaged through her bulging purse, pulled out a cellular phone, and punched in the number of her friend Cathy McGinnis. Anne and Cathy had been friends literally all their lives, and Cathy had proven her loyalty dozens of times through the years. "Hey, when're you going to leave? Okay. I'll be right on the schedule we talked about. See you at the hotel for dinner." Another glance at her watch. 3:25.

Anne proceeded to the automobile dealership that was the only source of rental cars in Jasper, Tennessee. Earlier that day, she had called to ascertain which car she would be taking. She spotted the nondescript compact, loaded her luggage into the back seat, and checked the mileage. She mentally added 85 miles to the odometer reading and walked into the dealership.

Inside, she spotted Howard Hall, a former high school classmate. "What brings you to our humble business? Can I fix you up with a real American car?"

"No, I'm just picking up a rental car to take to a conference in Nashville. Sorry—I'm running late and I have to go by the house, so I won't have time to make any big purchases."

"He-e-e-y!—big social worker meeting in Nashville, huh? Always glad to see our tax dollars at work." Howard smiled and pointed her in the direction of the clerk as he turned to greet a young couple walking in the front door.

Anne approached the cashier's window and found the girl who handled the rentals. "I'm Anne-Marie Atkins and I'm here to pick up the rental car that I spoke with you about earlier."

"I'll get your paperwork, Ms. Atkins." She left the window and walked to a two-drawer filing cabinet labeled 'Rentals' which also served as home for a close-to-death fern and a coffee maker. "By the way, I've already put my things in the car, and I checked and wrote down the mileage before I came in to save some time. I've got to go by my house first and I'm running late to get to a meeting in Nashville."

Anne repeated the story about going home, although she had no intention of going there, to make sure she was heard. She got the keys to the rental car, left the keys to her car, and hurried off. She waved to Howard who still had the young couple in tow.

Checking the mirrors of the car as she left the dealership, she turned north toward Nashville. Heavy clouds had turned to rain. She turned on the wipers and the heater and settled into the car. It seemed cozy in her own little world. The rain somehow seemed appropriate to her mission. If anything, it would help explain any delays along the way.

She was driving as fast as possible, but being careful. A speeding ticket would ruin everything. After a few minutes she pulled off alongside the road, cut off the engine, took the cellular from her purse and called her husband, Ron, at work.

"I just stopped by the house to pick up my clothes and a few things to take with me on the trip. I wanted to say goodbye before I headed off to my meeting." She made sure her voice sounded normal.

"Okay—don't worry about anything at home."

"Thanks a lot. I love you. Give the boys a kiss for me tonight."

"Don't worry about that. Why don't you give us a call before you go to bed? And be careful."

"Okay, bye."

She replaced the phone, which Ron did not know she had, in her purse and sped off toward Nashville. "Okay," she thought, "Ron could say that I had gone by the house."

Forty minutes later, she pulled off the Interstate at a convenience market. She bought some snacks and orange juice, making sure she got a receipt for her purchases, which she stuffed into her purse.

As she started out the door, she tossed the bottle of juice she had just purchased to the floor. The bottle was light and shattered instantly.

"I'm sorry. I can't believe how clumsy I am."

The clerk scrambled around the counter. "That's okay, honey. I just hope you didn't get anything on you."

"No, it looks like I managed to get it all over your floor, though. Let me help clean it up."

"That's okay, that's what they pay us for. I'll take care of it."

"At least let me help with the worst of it." Anne lingered to talk for a few minutes. She was sure, that if asked, the clerk could verify that she was between Jasper and Nashville at just the time she needed to be. The first part of the plan, the easy part, had gone off without a hitch. She got back in the car and drove back toward the Interstate. The signs pointed one way to Nashville and the other way to Chattanooga. Anne took a right, heading back the way she had come, toward Chattanooga.

* * *

"Hey, Jack!

"Well, if it isn't my colleague, Dr. Martinsen."

"And how was everything in orthopedics today?"

"Pretty good, thanks. I did a C-4 and a rotator cuff. How about yourself?"

"Office day—just coming by for a minute to see a patient. You got time to hit a few tennis balls? One of the indoor courts is available."

"No, sorry-big dinner plans."

"Too bad. Say hello to Myra for me. Assuming, of course, that you're dining with her."

Jack chuckled. "Good assumption. See you later."

He continued down the hall and into the physician's lounge on the surgery wing. He opened his locker, removed a silk sport coat, and slipped it on. He checked for his keys in his coat pocket, turned to a mirror, combed his close-cut, dark hair, and left the lounge. He stopped at the nurse's station on the surgical wing to make his final chart entries for the day and then left the wing headed for a rendezvous he could have never imagined.

* * *

It was 5:45 and drizzling rain as Anne pulled into the parking garage at West Side Hospital in Chattanooga. She made her way through the garage and found a space two floors below the entrance level to the hospital. The garage was dimly lit. Few people were coming and going. Everything was just the way she had remembered. She parked next to one of the end walls so she could open her door and not be seen.

Quickly pulling on a dirty old shirt and a pair of baggy men's overalls, she swirled her hair on top of her head and covered it with a baseball cap. Making sure that no one was around, she exited the car.

A casual observer would not have noticed that she was a woman dressed in farmer's clothing. The baggy shirt and overalls hid her slender female figure and the outfit definitely looked male.

The garage contained a series of steps that allowed her to make her way to the physicians' parking area quickly and unnoticed. She spotted the red Porsche and sighed with relief when she noticed that it was not parked close to a light. She crouched in the shadows beside the vehicle, pulled on a pair of surgical gloves, and waited. Minutes passed slowly and the tension mounted. Leaning up against the cold, hard concrete wall, she felt the bulky overalls pressing into the flesh of her back. Still, she waited.

*   *   *

Jack Kilday left the nurse's station on the physician's elevator and rode to the level where he had left his car. The elevator let him off into a small foyer. To his right was a walkway which led to the visitor's entrance to the hospital. Jack walked straight ahead through a single door toward the physician's parking lot.

As he entered the garage he paused for a moment and took in the smells of the outside world. It was raining. The odor of exhaust fumes filled his head, replacing the antiseptic odors of the hospital. He relaxed a bit as he left the medical world and entered reality.

Absorbed with his evening plans, he did not notice the scruffy figure crouched behind his vehicle. The figure waited until Kilday extracted his keys from his pocket.

At that instant, the figure rose from the shadows, holding a .22 caliber pistol with a silencer. She looked him in the eyes. It was important that he know who she was. Hatred shot from her eyes like laser beams, as if to lock the pistol onto the target. The gun coughed three times as three slugs entered Kilday's abdomen. Kilday cursed, stared in astonishment, and slumped to the floor of the garage. The figure coolly walked over to the body, pumped two more rounds into Kilday's head, removed his wallet, and returned to the shadows of the parking garage. She took the cash out of the wallet, and threw the wallet into a corner behind another car.

Leaving the area of the crime, the figure slipped back into the shadows, down two floors, and into the waiting rental car. She was safe. She slipped out of the overalls, and threw them in the back seat.

Anne started the car, drove out the bottom exit of the parking garage, and turned on to one of Chattanooga's busy streets, heading toward Nashville. She was careful not to exceed the speed limit. At 9:00 p.m. she met Cathy in the lobby of the Opryland Hotel and they proceeded to Jack Daniel's Restaurant for a late meal.

Cathy did not know where Anne had been between the time she left her job and the time they met at the hotel. If anyone asked, she was sure that they had met about 7:30 in the lobby, browsed through the shops in the complex, walked through the huge atrium at the hotel, and finally decided to have dinner about 9:00.

CHAPTER 2

▼

Anne awoke in a daze from a heavy, restless sleep. The combination of late nights and sleeping pills always produced a mind thickening fog when the alarm called in the early morning hours. She partially tossed back the covers and felt the coolness of the morning on her slender, bare legs. She felt in the darkness to see if Ron had left the bed. The mental fog was lifting slightly and she rolled over. Ron was gone.

Anne rolled back over, dropped one leg to the floor, propped herself up on one elbow and listened to an unknown country performer sing one of a hundred sound-alike songs that Chattanooga's biggest station belted out around the clock.

As the fog continued to lift, Anne slowly set into process the daily drag of getting ready for work. When both feet hit the floor, the heavy black cloud that had disappeared into the night descended and engulfed her body. For almost a year she had carried the cloud with her. She had no hope that it would go away.

She realized that she had again dreamed of carrying out one of her schemes for killing Jack Kilday. Over the past year she had been making plans for Kilday's death. Her ability to devise these complex, nefarious schemes was surprising. As she continued to awake from the intense dream, that moments before had seemed entirely real, she was further surprised that she was completely calm. She realized that she had not dreamed about how she would discard the pistol and clothing.

Half awake, she thought back over the problem of the gun and clothing. She could not dispose of them at the hotel. She couldn't risk throwing them out along the road to Nashville. Keeping the clothes would be too risky, and she couldn't just give them to Cathy. Forcing herself to return to reality, she made a mental note to go over this unresolved part again.

As she returned to a functioning level, she thought about the things she needed to do to get ready for the upcoming day. It was Thursday morning—a school morning. She went through a mental checklist of the boy's clothes which were clean and available for them to wear that day.

She dragged herself to the shower, adjusted the water to run as hot as she could stand, slipped off her gown, and felt the burn of the shower on her body. The combination of the hot water and her increasing mental capacity caused her pulse to quicken.

The black cloud opened to pour out some of its poison and she slammed the side of the shower with her hand. She had fallen into a dark hole. There was no bottom, no end, and she did not know where she was going or when it would stop. She only knew that when she hit the bottom, it was going to be a lot worse than it had been. She missed the world above and the life she had known.

Shaking her head, as if to shake away the cloud, she opened the shower door, and emerged into the coolness of the early morning. Cold and shivering, she stood naked in the dark, wondering what lay ahead. She reached for a towel, pushed aside the darkness in her mind, and plunged ahead into the day.

CHAPTER 3

▼

The Atkins farm is situated about a mile and a half from the Interstate just outside of Jasper, in Marion County, Tennessee. Ron and Anne had been married almost twenty years. Ron had landed a middle management position job with Evans Manufacturing, a local manufacturer of office furniture.

It was twelve years before they had children. Chad came first, and Alan followed after a two year interval. Now Chad was in second grade and Alan was in kindergarten. It had been a hassle with Anne trying to work while the boys were at home, but she had finally made it to the time when both boys were in school.

Anne shuffled into the kitchen, poured a cup of coffee, and fixed some dry toast. She sat in the dark for a few minutes. Then she took a deep breath, and like a child preparing to face punishment, turned and started down the hall to get the boys ready for school.

Anne walked into Chad's room, shook him to get him awake, and walked to his closet. She took one of his shirts out of the closet, held it up and said, "Is this what you want to wear today?"

Chad rolled over in bed, shook his head and mumbled, "No."

Anne pointed to the closet. "You go ahead and pick out what you want." She turned, walked to the chest in Chad's room, opened a drawer, and set out underwear and socks. As she left the room, she looked at her watch, made a concerned face and said, "We're running a little behind. You need to hurry up."

Anne left Chad's room and looked in on Alan. He was up and getting dressed. The boys would only have time for a quick breakfast so she had set out cereal, bowls, and spoons on the kitchen table.

Anne dropped Chad and Alan at Jasper Elementary School and drove to her job at the Marion County Health Department. She had several home visits to make that day and remembered that Chad was scheduled for a therapy session in Chattanooga at 5:30 P.M. She hated the late afternoon drives to Chattanooga. By then she was exhausted from worry, lack of sleep, and work. She felt guilty for dreading the sessions because she knew she had to pursue anything that held even the most remote glimmer of hope for Chad.

CHAPTER 4

▼

The telephone answering machine message clicked off and Ron heard Karen Holland, one of Anne's friends. "Hey Anne, it's Karen, give me a call…" He reached over from his recliner and picked up the phone.

"Hello, Karen. How you doin'?"

"Hi, Ron. Doing pretty well, if those brats over at the Middle School don't drive me crazy. How're y'all getting along?"

"'Bout half."

"Hang in there—things are gonna get better. Is Anne busy?"

"Let me see if I can find her."

Karen could hear Anne's footsteps on the way to the phone. "Hey Karen—about time I heard from you. Where've you been lately?"

"Oh, just around. Trying to hide from the kids I'm supposed to be counseling—you know the feeling."

"Gosh—some of those people that we're supposed to be working with—I swore to myself that I would never be one of those crazy mothers like we have to work with—but I tell you what, I think I'm becoming one of the worst. I'm about to drive some of Chad's therapists up the wall."

"By the way, how's Ron doing? He sounded terrible when I talked with him a minute ago."

"He's just about shut down emotionally. I swear that man has suppressed ever feeling he ever had in his whole life, and now he's just not able to deal with it."

"Have you thought about the two of you going to therapy?"

"Ha. There's the joke of the century. He'd rather die than go to therapy—and I mean that. He's taken to wandering around the farm at 4:00 o'clock in the morning and spending hours out in the barn. Fifteen years we've lived here and he's never had to work that much in the barn before. I guess in a way it's therapeutic."

"I'm sure it is, but he needs to find some way to let it all out."

"Listen—I hope he can't hear—but I went out to the barn a couple of evenings ago, and I swear he was just sitting up in the loft—I didn't hear a sound in the whole barn—and when I yelled for him, he came down, and I'm sure he'd been crying."

"Amazing—there's some real progress. I guess everybody looks at Ron as the strong silent type."

"He may be, but on the inside, I know he's dying. I mean, I can understand where he's coming from. You can't help but worry if Chad's going to be able to get along in the world, or if he's going to make friends. I swear, it kills me to think about him not being able to keep up with the other boys his age, and I'm sure it's worse for Ron—with sports and everything."

"Oh, yeah. Let's not forget about sports. I'm glad I don't have to put up with all that guy stuff."

Ron had fallen asleep in his recliner in the den. Anne's analysis of his condition was accurate. Both Ron and Anne felt a burden of guilt for Chad's illness. It was inevitable that they would feel that circumstances would be different if only they had acted differently. Rational minds could point out that they had done everything possible. In fact both of them had far exceeded the characteristic response of parents in the situation they faced. At times, their minds could accept this rational conclusion. However, the old darkness of guilt and shame always crept up from within.

Occasionally, Ron would awake from a fog at work and realize that he had been day-dreaming about Chad's future. The incessant burdens that he carried were affecting him emotionally, psychologically, and physically. He found it increasingly difficult to function at work and this brought on a completely new layer of worries.

Ron's only guidance in dealing with the crushing pain was something he remembered his father saying at the time of the death of his grandfather.

"Sometimes you just have to hunker down and take what life brings, I suppose," Ron recollected his father saying.

Ron had been running on automatic pilot, just "hunkered down" for almost a year.

CHAPTER 5

"What's the status of that Atkins situation?" bellowed Edwin Fellers, the managing partner of West Side Orthopedic Associates. The occasion was the weekly partners meeting. The doctors gathered at 7:00 each Tuesday morning to partake of coffee and doughnuts and discuss business. The Chad Atkins case had been a topic of discussion, off and on, for almost a year.

"I spoke to Wes Howell yesterday and he told me that there probably isn't anything we can do but wait and see if a lawsuit is filed," responded Hunter Hollings, the youngest member of the group.

Jack Kilday fidgeted. "I just don't like waiting around to see what some bunch of clods are going to do to screw up my life. I don't see why we can't go over there and offer them a little money just to get rid of the thing."

"Wes said there is a likelihood of stirring them up, in which case they might get the bright idea to go see a lawyer," responded Hollings.

Fellers had put on his down-to-business look. "Jack, did you get in touch with your friend in New Haven to see what he had to say about the case?"

"I talked to him three or four days ago and he said the general spread of infection sounds as good as anything to him," replied Jack, refocusing on the matter at hand.

"I'm willing to go with that if everybody else is," said Fellers, as the group nodded in silent accord.

Kilday noticed that Hollings appeared reluctant and shot him an icy stare. Kilday had never particularly cared for Hollings. He seemed too pious for Kilday's tastes.

"Just wait until one of his cases takes a bad turn and see how he feels," Kilday thought.

*   *   *

Jack Kilday never had a disappointing result in anything in his life. Growing up, if there was anything he couldn't do better than everybody else, he just didn't give it a shot. He had been valedictorian of his high school class in Cincinnati, done his undergraduate work at Ohio State, and attended medical school at Duke.

He did his internship and residency in Boston. While there he met his wife, a journalism student at Boston College, and they had decided to settle in her hometown of Chattanooga. Chattanooga was a step below Jack's expectations; however, he managed a tolerable lifestyle and had even come to enjoy the slower southern pace.

The fact that less-talented classmates had landed better positions in bigger cities was an annoyance to Jack. He nurtured his ego by writing in medical journals and establishing himself as one of the up-and-coming young orthopedic surgeons in the South.

At Ohio State Jack had played on the tennis team, and he was still one of the better players in the city. He had maintained his slim waistline and lean appearance. He and his wife had become absorbed in the best social circles in Chattanooga. He drove a new sports car and his wife a new luxury sedan in which she carted around their two children. Everything was going great for Jack Kilday, until the Chad Atkins case.

Sometimes Jack wondered what people expected. His was a profession of complex and intense judgment calls. Occasionally people died.

But let one patient get a bad result and some money-grubbing lawyer would be out to destroy him.

Jack resolved to do anything necessary to prevent that. He concluded that his job was to practice medicine, give everything he had to his patients, and try to maintain a semblance of a personal and family life. He was not going to allow this disgruntled patient to wreck his career over something that was inevitable.

*   *   *

"Well," roared Edwin, "we've had a few of these claims before and we'll either roll over them or throw them a few bucks and make the whole thing go away. And then life goes on."

"Sure," thought Jack, "life goes on for you."

Jack seethed as he remembered Anne's bitter eyes directed at him the one time they had met since Chad's surgery. "This woman has read a couple of articles and she thinks she knows all there is to know about surgery," he thought. Jack had run into Anne in the hospital library shortly after the surgery. At the time, he didn't know why she was there, but now he knew. Her hatred had burned as if she had thrown acid on him. He hadn't known what to say and left without a word.

Jack could understand the Atkins' disappointment with their son's illness. After all, he had kids of his own. "But I didn't give the kid the infection and I did everything within my power to care for him. Nobody can do the impossible," he thought. "Besides," he concluded in his mental argument with himself, "the medication theory he had discussed with his physician friend in New Haven seemed plausible."

Jack had gone through the make-believe trial of the malpractice case a dozen times in his mind. He had even gone so far as to make a list of the physicians who would testify in his behalf. He suspected the Atkins could find a physician somewhere to testify for them. He had heard that there were practitioners who were nothing more than prostitutes willing to testify for pay. "For enough money, I'm sure they can get somebody to say anything they want," he thought.

Jack reassured himself for the hundredth time that if a suit were to be filed, he could win. "Anyway, even if we lost the case, people would understand that it would be virtually impossible to overcome the sympathy that a jury would feel toward a child. People understand that this is just one of those things that happens to every doctor who is doing anything more than treating cuts and bruises."

Jack tried to put the whole matter out of his mind and ready himself to go to the hospital. "Somebody ought to do something. It limits the way I'm able to function," he thought as he made his way to the door.

CHAPTER 6

"Mrs. Atkins, could I speak with you for a few minutes," whispered Maurice Washington, a speech and hearing therapist who had been working with Chad since his hospitalization. Maurice was young but sincere in his work with Chad. Sincerity went a long way toward convincing Anne to continue with therapy even though the results were minimal.

"I don't know how to say this, and I hope you won't feel like I'm meddling in your business, but I feel like I ought to mention it. You know I'm not a medical expert, but I see a lot of patients come through here and I feel like you ought to check into the possibility of a lawsuit on Chad's case. If anybody asks, we never had this conversation, but I feel like we know each other well enough that I can talk to you. I don't know whether you'll get anything out of it, but I've talked with a lawyer who's a good friend of mine and he says there definitely is something there."

"What do you think went wrong?" Anne asked. Anne thought she knew some of the things that went wrong, but she wanted to hear it from someone in the medical field.

The thought of suing Jack Kilday excited Anne. In fact, the thought of suing Jack Kilday thrilled her almost as much as seeing him tumble off the top of a hundred story building would have thrilled her. She knew he had done something wrong and this confirmed it.

"Obviously you know I don't have a medical degree, but it doesn't take anybody too smart to figure out that Chad's condition didn't just happen," Maurice added.

"Do you really think we would have a good case?" Anne wasn't going to be put off. He knew something and she intended to find out what it was.

Maurice looked uncomfortable. "That's all I can tell you—I probably—I may have stepped over my bounds as it is. Whatever you do, don't tell a soul that I'm the one that suggested this to you."

"I swear I won't, but I really don't know who to see. I know a few lawyers in Marion County, but I really don't know whether any of them could take on something like this or not."

"I'd be glad to give my friend a call and try to set up an appointment."

Anne paused a moment, thinking the proposition over. "I don't know, I'd better check with Ron—you know, just to make sure—before we do anything."

"From what I understand you've got to file suit within a year of the time that this all happened, so you better not let too much time pass."

Anne gave Maurice a hug. "Gosh," she thought, "he was afraid to mention this to me, and this is the best news I've heard in months."

On the drive back to Jasper, Anne's mind was spinning. She decided to call her cousin, Johnny French, who worked at one of the town's banks. He had experience in dealing with lawyers and he might have some idea of lawyers to call. At the least he could give some advice. Despite the fact that Anne was thankful for the information, she wondered how many times he had done this in the past for his friend. "Maybe this guy is just some shyster who squeaks out a living settling cases that his buddy sends over to him," she thought. At least Johnny would have some way of checking up on him and maybe finding out who the best lawyers were to handle the case.

In any event, she was excited about her new information. Surely Maurice knew something that he couldn't tell her. She'd read Chad's hospital records and gathered all the information she could, but there had to be something that Maurice had heard through the hospital grapevine. She knew it was there and she knew if she could just find the right source, she'd find out what it was.

She was careful not to breathe a word to Chad. She didn't know how he would react to the filing of a lawsuit claiming that he had something wrong with him. She expected Ron to be skeptical. She knew he didn't trust lawyers or anything that he didn't fully understand. Anne had no idea how much it would cost to hire an attorney, but she knew it was going to be a bundle. She didn't care if it took everything they had, she intended to sue Jack Kilday.

She pictured Kilday on the witness stand squirming and sweating in his buttoned-up, prim and proper way. She imagined the lawyer tearing him limb from limb. "He might even get a wrinkle in his lab coat," she mused. The more she thought about it, the more she felt it would be worth everything she had just to see him on the witness stand explaining what he had done to her son.

CHAPTER 7

Anne could scarcely control herself through supper and the evening. She was dying to tell Ron about her conversation that afternoon and her thoughts in the meantime. As soon as she could, she hurried the children off to bed and they sat down in the den.

"Maurice Washington told me that he felt like we ought to sue Dr. Kilday." Anne was careful to overstate the conversation a bit to make sure that she caught Ron's interest.

"Isn't that the speech therapist? What does he know about lawsuits is what I'd like to know? I mean that's well and fine to pick up some kind of gossip around the hospital and get people all excited, but he isn't a doctor—or a lawyer either for that matter, and I have a hard time believing that he knows that much about lawsuits."

"He said he'd talked to a lawyer friend of his and the lawyer said we had a good case."

Ron paused. His black hair was now speckled with gray. When he was deep in thought, Anne had noticed he had a wise countenance that discouraged disagreement.

"Right, I'm sure that's a cozy deal. I wonder how much of a kickback he gets for every case? I'm just not sure I want Chad's name splashed all over everywhere and everybody coming to see a trial about all the

Atkins' troubles. We've got enough to worry about without some dang lawyer coming in and screwing things up."

"It wouldn't hurt to check around a little bit. I thought I'd call Johnny and see if he had any ideas about who we might talk to."

"What does Johnny know? He works at the bank. He's not a lawyer. Just because he deals with lawyers from time to time doesn't make him an expert on the law."

"I'm not saying that he's an expert on the law or anything like that, but he might know somebody we could talk to that would get us headed on the right track. I'm sure there are plenty of lawyers that could give us an idea whether we've got a case."

"I don't see what good it's going to do—it's only going to stir things up again."

Anne decided to let it drop. They both knew that she was going to call Johnny unless she got struck by lightning before she could get to the phone. Ron's grumbling was his way of slowing her down before she did something rash.

"I'll think about it," she said, as she walked out of the room, up to the kitchen, and to the phone.

With all of Ron's stated negativism, he was also excited about the possibilities. However, he had enough dealings with lawyers through his job to know that filing a lawsuit was a major step. He wasn't sure if he wanted to spend everything they had just to go up against the American medical establishment.

He turned the television on and settled back to look at the newspaper. He knew Anne would come walking down the steps in about an hour or so and fill him in on what Johnny had said. He would have been disappointed if she hadn't.

Anne had already gotten Johnny on the phone. "Listen, I talked to one of the therapists over at the hospital in Chattanooga. He told me that based on what he'd heard at the hospital, although he couldn't tell me exactly what it was, he thought we had a good lawsuit against one of the doctors." She waited expectantly for Johnny's evaluation.

Johnny seemed eager. "You know, from what you've told me before, that thought had occurred to me. I mean, things like that just don't happen unless somebody is responsible. They could have avoided what happened. So what do you need to do, locate somebody to handle the case for you?"

"This therapist at the hospital said he knew a lawyer in Chattanooga who handled these kinds of cases and he can get me an appointment with him. He didn't even give me his name and I really don't know how good he is, but he said he handles these kinds of cases."

Johnny thought for a minute. "I'd be careful about that. I know several lawyers and I'd be glad to check around to see who they think might handle the case for you."

"I sure wouldn't want a word of this to get out in town, so keep it quiet. Do you know any lawyers over in Chattanooga?"

"We've dealt with several of the firms over in Chattanooga so I know several people that I could check with, but the lawyers seem to generally know who handles what kind of case—probably some of them or some of the lawyers here in town could get us pointed in the right direction. Hmm, I'll tell you what I'll do, I'll call Sam Trestle. I might even be able to get hold of him tonight."

Johnny's wheels began turning. Sam Trestle had been a friend since first grade, and not only would Johnny like to help Sam out, but this would help firm up Sam's relationship with the bank. Nothing like scratching one another's backs to help everybody along.

"Do you think Sam Trestle can be trusted? You know I don't want him talking about this all over town to people—and anyway, I'm not sure I'd feel comfortable with him handling the case."

"I'm not saying I'd get Sam to handle the case—although I guess that's a possibility, but he probably would know somebody in Chattanooga, or maybe even somebody up in Nashville who handles these cases all the time. Sometimes the lawyers even help one another out, so maybe he could handle the case from this end, but get somebody to work with him."

"Johnny, I don't have a fortune to spend on this, you know, so I'd rather just find one person that could handle it without having to pay two or three lawyers."

Johnny's wheels continued to turn, only now a little faster. "I understand—and I'll just talk with Sam. I'm sure he'll keep it confidential and I'll either fix it up so you can talk with him, or I'll find out what he has to say."

He wanted to make it look like Anne's idea to have Sam handle the case. He knew darn good and well that Sam was going to want to handle the case. A case like this, with injuries like Chad's, would have to add up to some pretty big bucks. "I'll try to get back to you tomorrow and let you know. I'm not sure how long it'll take me to get hold of him."

Johnny knew how long it would take him to get hold of Sam—about ten seconds after he hung up with Anne. But he didn't want to appear too anxious or make it appear too easy.

Anne hung up the phone and walked cautiously back downstairs. She sat down in the easy chair and picked up a magazine.

"What did he have to say," Ron finally asked.

Anne smiled, knowing how easy she was to read. "He said he knew several lawyers over in Chattanooga in some of the big firms and he was sure that he could check confidentially to see who would be the best person for us to see. He can also check out this guy that Maurice knows, if we want him to." That wasn't exactly what Johnny had said, but it was close enough.

"So when's he going to check on this?"

"He said it might take a day or so, but he'd try to get on it tomorrow."

Ron went on to bed, and Anne sat alone, thinking about what to do. It was like this a lot. It was hard for her to sleep. She and Ron seemed to be on different wavelengths, as well as different schedules. On top of everything else she felt like she was losing Ron.

What about Sam Trestle? She used to think he was cute. He'd been several years ahead of her in school. What was it three years—four? She could vaguely picture him. Light brown hair, falling down on his forehead and just over his ears. He'd always had a somewhat boyish look, like a beach bum that had never quite settled down. He was about six-one, and giving way only slightly to the on-going middle-age calorie battle.

Would he be the kind of lawyer who was good at inflicting pain? How good was he? He'd been in with Horace Stoneham, so he must be okay. It would be good to have somebody local—he'd understand.

Okay, she thought, "I'll give Sam a try. Can't hurt to talk, I guess."

*   *   *

Johnny French didn't even bother to hang up the receiver when he got off the phone with Anne. He broke the connection and dialed Sam Trestle's number.

"Hello," a feminine voice answered.

"Hey good looking, is that no account husband of yours around?"

"Hi Johnny, I think he's around somewhere. Let me see if I can get him."

Johnny and Sam had known each other for years, and Lynn, Sam's wife, shook her head and ambled off toward the bedroom. She knew it would be late before he got off the phone. Sometimes he could be worse than a kid when it came to monopolizing the phone. She just hoped that somebody with something important to talk about wasn't trying to get through.

Sam padded to the phone, barefoot, wearing an over-sized T-shirt and an old pair of gym shorts. "Alright what do you want—you know we've got laws against libel and slander around here."

"I guess you wouldn't be talking that way to one of your oldest and best friends if you knew what he'd been trying to do for you. I swear I believe this is your lucky day—you been living right or what?"

Sam's and Johnny's down-home repartee had been polished over the years. "I try to make it a habit of living pretty close to right all the time so I guess you've hit the nail right on the head. Why—what's going on?"

"I just called to give you a lead on the best case you ever had and here you go talking about suing me for libel and slander." Johnny knew he had Sam's attention, but he savored the moment. "By the way—what were you doing that took so long to get to the phone?"

"We can talk about what I was doing later, I'd just like to hear about this big case. What do you need me to do, sue some guy on a hundred dollar note or something?"

"Yeah, right—You'll be handling plenty of hundred dollar cases for me after you get through with this one. Oh, and you might as well get ready to buy me a big steak dinner whenever I get ready."

"Are you gonna keep beating about the bush about what a great guy you are, or are you going to tell me why you called?"

Johnny's voice got more serious. "Listen, my cousin Anne called a few minutes ago and said that some guy over at the hospital in Chattanooga told her that he had some inside information about malpractice on her kid. You know—he was in the hospital last year—and all the problems they've been through—so this guy told her that he has some inside hospital information that they made a mistake or something. Anyway, she called me and wanted me to see what I could work out about talking to a lawyer. I told her I would check with you, but you might be too busy to get involved." Johnny allowed himself a chuckle.

"Anyway I'm going to steer her over to you if you want me to." Johnny could picture Sam's face across the phone line.

"Heck, yes, I'm interested,—she can come right on over tonight if she wants to."

"I don't think you ought to appear too anxious. This guy over in Chattanooga said he had some lawyer buddy that wanted to handle it, so you probably shouldn't get too excited."

"Yeah, he probably does have a buddy that he's making a good side income off of from these cases. Who is it, by the way?"

"She didn't have any names, and I pretty much tried to discourage her. I tried to use the buddy referral angle to scare her out of that idea, but I did tell her if you took the case you might want to get somebody over in Chattanooga or Nashville or somewhere to work with you."

"I don't know why you told her that. I've tried as many cases as any of those guys." Johnny paused a moment. "Do you have experience in really big cases?"

"Well, of course every case I handle isn't astronomical, but I've had my share." He thought for a second, had second thoughts, but then added, "You know, I've got that big one where the woman fell on the steps over at the shopping center."

"Yeah, I remember—of course you have to make all those decisions. Anyway, just keep your shirt on, I was just trying to smooth things out a little bit so that if she wasn't real thrilled about you handling the case—which she wasn't, by the way—she might at least cut you in on a little bit of the action. She told me pretty quick she didn't expect to hire two or three lawyers; she figured one would be about all she could afford."

"Ah, the fees are pretty much the same anyway. Just about everybody charges one-third of whatever is recovered, and if two, three, four or five lawyers are involved, they just split the fee. But, anyway I appreciate you giving me the lead."

CHAPTER 8

Sam was interested in the case; however, he had been practicing law in the hills of Southeast Tennessee long enough to know that everything that glittered on the surface was not gold. In the early years, he had chased enough rabbits through enough briar patches to learn that sometimes you never caught the rabbit, and sometimes the chase could be rather unpleasant.

As a young attorney he had taken several cases which held the promise of fame and fortune but ended up costing him hours of sweat with little or no payoff. He also knew that a case against a group of prominent doctors was not going to be easy.

It stung a bit that Johnny had questioned his ability to handle a big, complex case, partly because he knew that Johnny's concerns were warranted. He had been involved in some big cases, but always with some assistance. He wished he had not brought up his one current "big case," but it had come to mind as the best example of a big, tough case that he believed he would win. He hoped that a big verdict would help establish his reputation for handling the larger cases.

Sam had been in enough cases to know the pressures of carrying a client's burden through the lengthy process of trial. He had seen plenty of lawyers drop dead of heart attacks or give up the trial of serious cases. Sam was fortunate that Lynn understood the stress and strain of the life of a country lawyer. Many wives didn't, which also explained why a lot of lawyers dropped dead of heart attacks.

Sam walked into the family room of their old two story house on Seventh Street in downtown Jasper. Sometimes he wondered why Lynn insisted on calling it the "family room" since they had never been able to have children. The inability to have children had been a big disappointment to Lynn. Sam somehow felt like a failure.

Sam was one of a dying breed of small town country lawyers. Sometimes he and the other members of the Marion County Bar, all eight of them, when they were sitting at the courthouse waiting for a jury to come in, or in one of the other all too often delays in the legal process, would talk about the turn for the worse that the practice of law had taken.

Sam loved those times. The hours would occasionally drag on, seemingly forever, while they waited for the jury to come in. You never knew when they were going to come back or what they were going to say. Sam felt that after all was said and done, their decision was usually closer to the truth than the lawyers wanted to admit.

Sam loved what he did. In the twenty years since he had started practicing law in Marion County, he had seen tremendous changes in the legal system. It was difficult to practice by himself in a profession that was becoming much more highly specialized. In the larger cities, the lawyers clustered in huge firms. Some of the larger firms in Tennessee had merged to form state-wide legal kingdoms. Even in rural Marion County, there were now two law firms composed of practitioners who had been, until recently, engaged in solo practice. Specialization was the name of the game and Sam was still a general practitioner.

His practice consisted of representing the local townsfolk in various squabbles, writing wills and handling estates, a few legal matters for the bank where Johnny worked, divorces, DUI's and various other minor legal matters. He had been county attorney for several years before one of the local firms had out-politicked him. The firm had offered Sam a job and the opportunity to continue with some of the county work, but Sam had turned them down. He enjoyed his independence and the freedom to do what he wanted, when he wanted, without having to answer to a group of partners.

Sam grew up in South Pittsburgh, the other small town in Marion County. His father was a foreman at the Evans plant, and his mother died when he was six. He and his brothers and sisters had the benefit of a solid middle class upbringing in a small southern town. Sam had five brothers and sisters, four of whom still lived in the Marion County area. Sometimes he figured that if all else failed, he had enough of a built-in clientele with his brothers and sisters to scratch out a living.

Sam's upbringing had been rough at times, without a mother. He had been practically raised by an older sister. His father never remarried and seemed always to be at work at the plant. His father did the best he could, but the kids were more or less on their own.

Lynn, Sam's wife, taught physical education at South Pittsburgh High School. They had tried for years to have children without success and finally gave up when they both turned forty.

They had never been well off, including their years with Sam practicing law and Lynn teaching. Sam learned early on that practicing law in a rural county was not a ticket to wealth. Sam's practice generated little regular income. Occasionally he would have a big fee, which usually got gobbled up by outstanding bills or buying equipment for the office. Sam actually enjoyed the challenge of the ups and downs of the finances, and although Lynn didn't enjoy it, she had learned to live with it.

Sam and Lynn had always liked the old white two-story house in Jasper, and when it became available through an estate sale, they had scraped up every nickel they could get their hands on and bought it. It remained in basically the same condition as when they had purchased it fifteen years ago. Sam liked the old house and enjoyed being able to walk to and from work. The house was only four blocks from his office.

Sam drove an older model Jeep which came in handy for hunting, fishing, and golfing, but when the weather allowed, he preferred to walk to the office to get his juices flowing.

Days seldom started on any kind of schedule for Sam. Some mornings he was at the office when the sun came up, and some mornings he didn't come in until 10 o'clock. He realized he could not do this at a large firm.

Sam also relished carrying on the tradition he had inherited from Horace Stoneham, a fixture of the Marion County Bar for many years, who had taken Sam in right out of law school.

Sam had few breaks in life and had to work for those he had gotten. His one big break came when Horace Stoneham inquired if Sam would like to practice with him. Sam recognized a good opportunity when he saw one and made the most of the opportunity.

Horace Stoneham's reputation as a lawyer only slightly exceeded his reputation as a character in Marion County. He had, unfortunately, over the years developed the habit of drinking excessively.

Sam had heard the story dozens of times, and always laughed and nodded as if it were the first. Years ago, one Marion County resident in need of a lawyer had inquired, "Who's the best lawyer in Marion County?"

"Horace Stoneham, when he's sober," came the response.

"So who's the second-best?"

"Horace Stoneham when he's drunk, I reckon."

Sam wondered if Horace hadn't started the story. Whether initiated by Horace or not, it had become part of the lore of Marion County, and Sam still benefited from it.

Sam and Horace had practiced together until Horace died in a Marion County courtroom five years before. All in all, Sam figured that was as good a way to go as any. Horace died waiting on his last jury to come in. Folks around Marion County still talk about the day that old Horace tried his last lawsuit, sat in his usual seat at the bar in the

Marion County courthouse, and fell over dead. Horace was never one to do anything in the normal way.

CHAPTER 9

▼

The Downtown Cafe is situated on the Court Square in the heart of Jasper. Three hundred and sixty-five days each year it opens its doors at six a.m. and serves as a gathering spot for locals looking for coffee, breakfast or conversation. Contacts are made, deals are done and elections are won or lost at the Downtown Cafe.

Johnny French, the most regular of the regulars, has his own table, which usually includes several real estate agents, lawyers and insurance agents. Part of his job is eating breakfast and keeping tabs on the pulse of Marion County every morning. He was at his usual perch in the back corner, where he could see everyone in the place when the door opened and Sam Trestle walked in. Sam eyed Johnny, grabbed a cup of coffee and headed for the back.

"Well, well—you're out and about awfully early. You don't usually get going 'till 8:30 or 9:00."

Johnny gave Sam a wry grin and kicked a chair away from the table. Also seated around the table were Bud Wilson, who worked with Johnny at the bank, and Ralph Dyson, a realtor.

"Something wrong with a guy gettin' a cup of coffee?"

"Thought you might have something else on your mind."

"Let's talk about it later—you didn't hear anything did you?" Sam didn't mind Johnny's attempt at humor, but he didn't want Ralph or

Bud to get wind of the case. If word got around, Ron and Anne might conclude that he was the source of the leak.

"It's only 8:00 in the morning—I'll call a little later."

Dyson's curiosity was aroused. "Call who? You guys got something going on?"

"Lawyer stuff—don't worry about it." Sam gave Johnny a look. "Could we talk about something else?"

"Sure," replied Dyson. "How 'bout golf?"

"Golf. That works for me. We gonna play Saturday?"

"Saturday morning, 9:15."

"Sounds good to me."

Sam put down his coffee cup and looked at Johnny, who had put on a serious face for the moment. "Don't worry about it—it's in the bag—just don't get over anxious."

Sam tossed a dollar on the table and started for the door. As he walked out, Sam remembered Johnny's warning. "Don't want to be under anxious either," he thought, "If you don't speak up, the next thing you know all you have left is the good feeling that you didn't appear too anxious, and that doesn't buy a whole lot of groceries."

Getting clients and cases was important business and Sam intended to make it the focus of his business until he had the case in hand. About 8:45 Alma, Sam's secretary, walked in the office. Alma had been Horace's secretary "since the memory of man ranneth not to the contrary" as Horace used to say. Since Alma had been working in the office for considerably longer than Sam, a casual observer might wonder who was the boss. Alma generally came and went as she saw fit, but she usually worked more than the forty hours for which Sam paid her.

As soon as she came in, Alma knew something was up. Sam relayed his conversation with Johnny of the night before.

"Do you think you'll get the case?"

"Johnny says it's in the bag, but you never know."

Part II

▼

"Just because you're paranoid doesn't mean they're not out to get you."
Sign in attorney Bill Hawkins' office, circa 1976.

CHAPTER 10

▼

It was a very complex, multi-faceted puzzle. Anne had only gotten tiny pieces of information at the time and they hadn't fit together. Looking back at the big picture, most of it made sense. But she hadn't been able to put it together at the time.

That was one of the things that made her so mad. Mad at herself. Mad at Kilday. Mad at the world. Mad at God. Guilty. She felt guilty. And stupid. And mad.

She could remember the first thing, just like it was yesterday. Remember right where she was sitting, what she was wearing—what it felt like, smelled like, looked like.

It was one of the first really nice days of spring. Anne was sitting in the bleachers at the little league field with a diet soda in one hand and the last of a hot dog with chili in the other. She remembered the chili running down her fingers, and how the warmth of the sun felt on her face.

She screamed as Chad rounded first on his way to second. Chad's team was losing and Chad had hit the ball into the outfield. As the outfielders scurried to relay the ball to third base, Chad rounded second. Chad and the ball arrived at third at approximately the same time. Chad turned to his right, slowed down and eased his way into the base where he was tagged out to end the game.

The parents on Anne's side of the field groaned. She found it difficult to understand why Chad had slowed down at the last minute. His half-hearted attempt to avoid the tag was puzzling.

After the game, she and Ron helped load up the bats, balls and equipment and started toward the family pickup. "You seemed to slow down a little bit when you went into third, Chad. That's not like you."

"I don't know. It didn't seem like I was going to make it, and my shoulder's hurting."

"Why's your shoulder hurting? I don't remember you getting hit or anything."

"I don't remember either. I—I don't know, it just kinda started feelin' sore."

"When we get home we'll put the heating pad on it and maybe that'll help. We've got to get you ready to play the next game."

When they got home, Anne got the heating pad, adjusted the heat and made Chad sit down with it on his shoulder. After ten or fifteen minutes he assured her that it was better.

After the boys were asleep, Anne thought about the shoulder again. "It sure seems weird about Chad's shoulder. I don't think I've ever seen him slow down doing anything. I guess it's just one of those things that'll go away in a day or two."

"I sure hope so," Ron said, his head buried in the sports section.

The next day Chad's team played again. "You know my shoulder is still kinda hurting. I hope it doesn't mess up my hitting."

"Maybe we ought to get it looked at," Anne said. "You hadn't said anything and I thought it had gotten better. If it really gets to bothering you, let me know. I don't want you playing if there's a chance you could get hurt." The game passed without incident and in the glow of victory Ron and Anne forgot about Chad's shoulder.

The following day Anne reached over to give Chad a hug and he drew back as if in anticipation of pain. "What's wrong honey?"

"Aw, that shoulder is still hurtin'. I don't know—it seems to be hurting more."

"I'm going to call Dr. Truelove's office first thing in the morning and see if Judy has any idea about it. Now, until then, you go in there and put the heating pad on that shoulder again."

"Aw, its not all that bad."

"I don't care, I want you to get that heating pad on that shoulder. You may not be able to play any more this year if we don't get it well." The latter threat seemed to be sufficient. Anne heard the heating pad click on just before the television.

Ron sauntered into the kitchen and grabbed a soft drink from the refrigerator. "So, what do you make of Chad's shoulder?"

"I don't know—probably just a sprain or something. I think I'll call Dr. Truelove's office in the morning and see if he thinks he needs to take a look at it."

"Good luck. Last time I called, I talked to Judy for about ten seconds, and she gave me some advice, and that was that."

"I know, sometimes I wonder if we ought to take the boys on over to one of the pediatric groups in Chattanooga. A lot of people do. It's just—I guess for some reason, I just trust him. He delivered me and just about everybody else in Jasper."

"Yeah, I guess I can't complain, Judy's advice worked."

"She ought to know about as much as he does by now."

"Maybe she does." They shared a chuckle.

"I'm gonna give them a call—at least I'll feel better."

* * *

It was late morning before Anne could get free to call the doctor's office. "Judy, this is Anne Atkins. Chad has a sore shoulder and I think he probably needs to be seen."

Judy took over and suggested the obvious. "Sometimes when those things get hit like that, it takes a lot longer for them to heal up than we would expect. Why don't you give him some Tylenol and put the heating pad on it. I suspect it'll start getting better in a day or two. If it doesn't, you let me know."

"He didn't say he hit it. He doesn't remember injuring it, and I don't remember anytime it got hit."

"Why, honey, I can't imagine it'd just start hurting all of a sudden. Why he probably just doesn't remember. Sometimes it can hurt later on for several days worse than it did at first. That'd be my guess. I'd say that he's banged it and just forgot about it and then slept on it the wrong way or something like that. You just try a little Tylenol and see if that doesn't help."

Anne-Marie gave up. She continued the Tylenol and heating pad. Two days passed with no particular change in Chad's shoulder.

The next day Anne was back on the phone. She explained that they had tried Tylenol, tried the heating pad, and nothing seemed to be helping.

Judy finally relented. "Why don't you bring him in this afternoon and we'll let Dr. Truelove take a look at him? I can't imagine why he isn't getting any better."

Anne left work, picked up Chad early from school and went by Dr. Truelove's office.

"Well, what have we got here Anne, a sore shoulder?" queried Dr. Truelove. "Seems as though I remember doctoring you for a few aches and bruises along the way. What's the matter—did he hurt himself playing ball, or what's going on?"

Anne explained the situation to Dr. Truelove emphasizing that no one, especially Chad, remembered anything at all about an injury to his shoulder.

"I don't know what to make of that, but we'll sure take a look at it and see what we can find." Dr. Truelove asked Chad to remove his shirt and probed along the left shoulder. He silently noted Chad's reaction to his probing. Do you have any other sore places or are you feeling bad any other way son?"

"No sir, just my shoulder."

"I think it might be good to take him on over to the hospital and get them to x-ray the shoulder. Sometimes just the slightest pull on some of the muscles or cartilages in that joint can result in real pain. I guess I don't have to tell you about that, do I?"

"No sir," replied Chad.

"Anne, you take Chad on over by the hospital and I'll call and have them make an x-ray and then call me first thing in the morning after I've had a chance to look at it. Maybe we'll know a little bit more."

CHAPTER 11

Anne could not help but feel concerned even though she told herself it was probably nothing. The next morning she hurried to work and called the doctor's office.

"Dr. George wants you to bring Chad back this morning. He said there appears to be some swelling around that joint and he would like to check it out a little more." Anne left work, picked up Chad and hurried to Dr. Truelove's office.

"I found some swelling around that shoulder joint," Dr. Truelove informed Anne in his slow drawl. "That could be caused by trauma to the shoulder which has resulted in inflammation and swelling. I suppose there's also the possibility that there could be some infection in the shoulder or the possibility of a growth which is just beginning. I'd have a hard time believing that it was either of those last two things, but I want to make sure."

Dr. Truelove informed Anne that he had made an appointment with an orthopedic group in Chattanooga. "It certainly won't hurt to have them take a look at it, and they may be able to pick up something we can't. I suspect they may want to make some more x-rays over there, but here are the ones from yesterday."

* * *

Anne was on edge as she drove Chad to Chattanooga. They found a parking spot and took the elevator to the eighth floor of the medical office building. As they entered the office of West Side Orthopedic Associates, Anne took in the plush, warm feel of the offices. She filled out the requisite insurance forms and was soon ushered back to a small examining room. "You certainly get quicker service here than with the doctors in Jasper," she thought, as her mind went back to hours of waiting in Dr. Truelove's office over the years.

They had waited only a few minutes when a young doctor with tortoise rim glasses and a crisply pressed lab coat came in. Anne couldn't help but notice his good looks, accentuated by his dark eyes.

"Hello, I'm Dr. Kilday," he said and extended his hand. Anne could have kicked herself as she felt her face light up. "And this must be Chad." He extended his hand to Chad and gave him a warm smile. Anne's comfort level increased considerably.

"Now, what's wrong with this guy. He certainly is a healthy looking customer."

Anne related the symptoms of Chad's shoulder. The doctor asked Chad to remove his shirt and went through the same tapping and probing on the shoulder that Dr. Truelove had done.

"We brought some x-rays that were made at the Marion County Hospital," Anne volunteered.

"Oh, I wasn't informed that you would be bringing films with you. Let me take a look." Although there was a viewing box in the examining room, he walked out with the x-rays. In a few minutes he returned.

"Based on the kind of equipment they are using over there, these films are awfully rough. I really can't tell much about them—and it's hard for me to see how they can provide quality care with that kind of equipment. I'm going to have to send him for some more x-rays and we may want to do a scan just to get a good picture of what's going on in the shoulder."

"Do you have any idea what could be wrong?" Anne felt the nervous energy begin to return.

"We make it a policy not to give any opinions until we're sure of what we are talking about. I think it's just unprofessional to speculate until we've done enough tests to be able to tell you for sure. I certainly don't want to lead you down the wrong pathway."

"We'll schedule with radiology for tomorrow. If you'll call my office first thing in the morning, we'll tell you the time. In the meantime, I'm going to prescribe some anti-inflammatory medications to see if we can get some of that swelling down. After we've had a chance to review the films, you'll hear from our office and we'll set up another appointment."

Anne began calling West Side Orthopedics at 7:00 a.m. the next morning. She finally reached someone an hour later. No, they did not know the time of Chad's appointment. They asked her to call back. As time passed Anne's anxiety increased. Ron passed it all off as much ado over nothing. "We see the same thing at the plant everyday. This is what causes these rising insurance costs. They have to run every test known to medical science before they tell you you've got a pulled muscle."

Finally, at 11:15, after four more telephone calls, Anne was told that x-rays could not be done until the following day at 8:30 A.M. She thought about trying to get in touch with Dr. Kilday to see if something couldn't be done to hurry things up but decided that if the time was not okay he would have done something himself.

Anne drove Chad to West Side Hospital in Chattanooga for x-rays the following day. The passage of time had not done anything for her level of concern. She kept telling herself that everything was okay.

The x-rays seemed to be a repeat of the ones which had been done at Marion County. However, she felt better knowing that the equipment at West Side was undoubtedly better than that at her small town hospital.

Anne returned Chad to school and when she returned home, found a message on the answering machine scheduling an appointment with Dr. Kilday at 4:00 p.m. the following Monday. She consoled herself with the thought that if anything was seriously wrong he would have wanted to see Chad immediately.

* * *

"Hey, how did it go with the doctor over in Chattanooga?" It was Cathy McGinnis, calling to check on Chad.

"Let's just say that if he can doctor as good as he looks, Chad would have been well before we left the office." Anne briefed Cathy on the details of her visit.

"I guess you're not exactly dreading the follow-up visit—hey, maybe I ought to go with you to offer some moral support."

"Oh, I think we'll do just fine. Besides he's married."

"Yeah? And so are you."

"Oh yeah."

Over the weekend Chad appeared less active than usual and Anne thought that he had a temperature. "Great," she thought, "on top of everything else he comes down with the flu." Finally, she and Chad traveled back to Dr. Kilday's office.

"I've looked at these films and see nothing to lead me to believe that this is anything other than a sprain." I know you don't remember any kind of traumatic incident; however, you would be surprised at the number of people I see for these kinds of injuries who don't remember anything that could have caused them. We see people with serious back injuries caused by simply sitting down or bending over. Did the anti-inflammatory medication make your shoulder feel better, Chad?"

Chad looked relieved. "I I think I'm better. I sorta felt like I had the flu or somethin' over the weekend—but I guess I'm okay."

"So you definitely feel like there isn't anything in there like a growth or anything?"

"No, I don't see anything of that nature. There is obviously swelling in the tissue around that shoulder joint, but I don't see anything of that nature."

"What I would like to do is continue you on those anti-inflammatories, and give you some pain medication which will make him feel better and which should also speed up the healing process. I think I'd also like to put the arm in a sling for about ten days and see if the immobilization of the arm doesn't speed up the recovery process."

Chad felt disappointed that he would not be able to participate in his normal activities, but proud of this emblematic badge of his injury.

"The nurse will bring you the prescriptions and help you put the sling on his arm, and I'd like to see you both back here in ten days."

Anne felt herself blushing again as Kilday put his hand on her shoulder. She was annoyed at herself for realizing that she was already looking forward to the return visit.

CHAPTER 12

▼

On Friday, Chad awoke complaining that he was feeling badly. Anne was sure she felt a temperature and left him at home until she could call Dr. Truelove's office. Chad assured her that his shoulder was feeling better. "At least we're getting one thing taken care of," she thought.

At 9:00 a.m., moments after Dr. Truelove's office had opened, she called Judy. Judy called back at 10:30 and advised that Dr. Truelove had phoned in a prescription.

"He probably has a touch of the flu," Judy said, "Dr. George was pleased to know that his shoulder is feeling better. I was pretty sure it was a sprain—we received a report from West Side Orthopedics yesterday."

"Does that report tell you the prescriptions that Dr. Kilday has given Chad?" Anne asked.

"Yes, honey—this won't interfere."

Anne left Chad in bed and ran to the pharmacy. She returned and found Chad asleep. She woke him up, gave him the first capsule and let him go back to sleep. She got her mother to sit with Chad and went on to the office.

Anne's mother told her that Chad slept most of the day. He didn't seem to have much of an appetite and complained of having a headache.

Ron was no help. "Why, I'm sure he'll be fine by the first of the week. Everybody gets these things and you just can't go running off to the doctor every time you have a headache or sick stomach." Chad went to sleep early on Saturday night. Anne stayed up and tried to read or watch TV, but could not get her mind on anything. By 1:00 a.m. she had resolved to get to the bottom of the situation. She decided to get him to see a doctor one way or another first thing Monday morning.

She couldn't escape the vague feeling that she was being overly protective. She knew from work how annoying an overly protective parent could be, and she had vowed that she would never cause that kind of problem to someone else. However, she resolved that she was going to find out what was wrong with Chad.

CHAPTER 13

Anne woke up on Sunday with the first rays of the sun. She had fallen asleep in Ron's recliner with the television staring at her. She made coffee, fixed a couple of pieces of toast, and paced in the kitchen until she could justify waking Chad.

She did so at 7:00 a.m. For a moment she thought that he was just having a difficult time waking up. After a few minutes, she realized that his mind wandered to the extent that he could scarcely wake up. Anne hurried to the bedroom and woke up Ron.

"I'm going to call mother and get her to watch Alan and I'm going to the emergency room. You can come on as soon as she gets here. I just think we both need to be there to deal with this."

Ron surprised her by suggesting that they go directly to Chattanooga. "I think we could probably get somebody who knows what they're doing over there, and since you've already seen a doctor there they may be able to call him in."

"I'm not sure we have time to get to Chattanooga. Maybe after we get him up and get him in the car, then we can tell."

Ron grabbed Chad up and carried him to the car. He was listless and limp. "I think you need to head on to Chattanooga right now. If you go over to our emergency room, they'll just tell you to give him a couple of aspirin and then send him on back home."

Anne slammed the door and roared out of the driveway. On the way down the highway, Chad awakened a bit and wondered where he was going in his pajamas in the car at 7:00 in the morning. Anne finally decided that Ron was right and headed up the interstate to Chattanooga.

She drove directly to West Side and found her way to the emergency room entrance. Two attendants appeared with a wheelchair and wheeled Chad inside. He remained in the wheelchair for what seemed like an interminable time while Anne answered questions. The young lady at the admitting desk finally said, "We've had an awful lot of flu in the last two weeks."

Anne jumped from the chair and threw the attendant's pen across the desk. "He doesn't have the flu. I've been going through this for two weeks and I know my own son. I can tell you for sure, he doesn't have the flu and I want to find somebody that can tell us what he does have." The nurse picked up the phone and turned her back to Anne.

Two nurses arrived for Chad and took him back to the treatment room. Anne assumed from their cold looks that they didn't want her to follow, but she didn't intend to let him out of her sight. Chad was wheeled back to a large examining room and lifted into a hospital bed that was surrounded by a curtain. Anne held his hand and waited.

In a minute, a young black man walked in. "Hi, I'm Dr. Wilcox. We need to take a look at your son and run a few tests."

"Listen, I'm tired of people looking at him and running tests. I can tell you he doesn't have the flu, and I can tell you he does have something that probably has to do with his shoulder." Her response had a little more bite than she had anticipated. She smiled slightly and looked down.

The doctor recoiled and gave Anne a slight smile. "Ma'am, there's not very much I can do if I don't take a look and run some tests. That's what we do. I'm sure you're upset but I'm going to do the best I can as quickly as I can, and we can get started and do it a lot quicker if you will sit down over there and let me do my job."

Anne took a seat, pleased to find somebody who wanted to get on with finding what Chad's problem was. She liked Dr. Wilcox. She suspected that the shoulder must have something to do with Chad's condition. Thoughts of cancer or other diseases were running rampant through her mind and she felt weak. She remembered that she had failed to tell Ron where she was going. She made a mental note to call him as soon as she had the opportunity, but she was not going to leave Chad now.

The doctor yelled for a nurse and one appeared almost instantly. "We need to set up a scan as quickly as we can and I need you to draw some blood while we're waiting."

Anne advised the doctor that Chad had already seen Dr. Kilday the previous week. "Try to get Dr. Kilday on the phone so we can bring him in on this situation," the doctor said as he exited the room.

Anne was left in the stillness with Chad. The room was cold and stark. The smell of antiseptic was heavy. She didn't know if she could stand it, but she did her best to walk to the bedside. She held his hand and felt tears coming to her eyes.

Moments later the nurse reappeared to take Chad's temperature and draw the blood. Thank God somebody was doing something, and they appeared to be doing it quickly. Anne felt that she was finally getting some attention to Chad's situation and although her anxiety level had heightened, she at least felt like she had the attention of someone who could do something.

Dr. Wilcox reappeared. "We've gotten Dr. Kilday's answering service and we've scheduled a cat scan. He has an elevated temperature, so we're going to proceed with the possibility that there may be some infection. As soon as we can get Dr. Kilday over here, I want to get his thoughts, but these tests need to be run." Anne felt somewhat relieved. Surely, they could do something if it was just an infection.

In a few minutes a bearded, long haired attendant appeared. "We're going to take him down to radiology. You can come along if you want to." They started down the long hallway leading from the emergency room with Anne closely following. The radiology department was one floor up and down a long corridor. The sounds of Anne's footsteps sounded ominous in the empty hallway. They entered radiology and Chad was picked up by a technician. "I'm sorry but you can't go back with him to the scan. If you'll just take a seat here we'll let you know as soon as he's through."

"But, I'm his mother. I won't be any bother, I'd just like to come along. I'm sure he'll want me to come along."

"I'm sorry ma'am but it's hospital policy. You'll just have to wait here."

The technician reappeared in about an hour. Anne was beside herself with worry. Surely it wouldn't have taken so long if they hadn't found something significant. "Can you tell me what you found or give me any idea of what's going on?" Anne asked. Her nervousness was increased by the fact that she had tried to reach Ron but found that he had already left home. Her mother told her he was en route to the hospital, but Anne realized that he probably wouldn't know which hospital.

"I'm sorry ma'am but we won't be able to tell anything until the radiologist has had a chance to look at the scans."

"Well, what kind of scans did you do?" Anne asked.

"The doctor ordered a routine cat scan and we'll let you know the results as soon as they are available," the attendant responded and as he started toward the door, Anne followed him back to the emergency room.

When they returned to the emergency room, the attendant advised Anne that Dr. Wilcox was admitting Chad. "We'll take him on up to a room as soon as possible. In the meantime, we're going to need to run a few more tests, and I'm going to need for you to wait outside," Dr. Wilcox informed her.

"I'm not about to leave him in here by himself. Whatever you need to do you can do with me in the room," Anne asserted.

"Now, Ms. Atkins, we've had this little talk once before. We're going to do the best we can, but we don't need you and any germs in the room. We can work a lot more efficiently if you'll just have a seat outside. There's not a thing in the world you can do. We just need to take some more blood and continue to monitor what's going on and there's not a thing in the world that you can do. It really would be better if you'll just let us do that and have a seat outside."

Anne drug back to the waiting area and joined several other expectant patients and their relatives. One of the Sunday morning "preacher shows" was on the television in the waiting area. She waited nervously for about thirty minutes and then saw Ron's car pull up outside.

"Thank goodness you finally got here. I had no idea if you would know where to come." She threw her arms around him and just held on for a few seconds in an attempt to re-energize herself.

"I remembered you had come here for the x-rays. So after I went by Marion County and you weren't there, I assumed that you probably came on here."

The mention of x-rays made Anne's mind start to run. "Would they have known about the previous x-rays? Why couldn't they just look at them rather than run the scans? They must expect something serious if they had to run the scan."

Anne tried to fill Ron in but realized that she knew very little. They walked in to the waiting area. In a few minutes the desk clerk called to Ron to get some more information. "She's probably too afraid to ask me," Anne reflected on the earlier pen throwing incident.

While Ron was filling out forms and giving insurance information, Dr. Wilcox appeared. He motioned to Anne.

"We're going to go ahead and move him up to pediatric intensive care. I think we can keep a better eye on him there and it will be easier for us to do any tests we need." Fear filled Anne's body.

"Well, what do you think it is?" Ron asked.

"You must be the father. I'm Dr. Wilcox," he said as he extended his hand. "We have no way of making a complete diagnosis at this time, but we're going to need to rule out any kind of infection. One reason I want him in PICU is so that we can keep a closer eye on him and run more tests to verify that possibility. If so, we'll start antibiotics as soon as possible."

Dr. Wilcox gave Ron and Anne directions to PICU on the fourth floor and both of them, filled with apprehension, started off in that direction. Neither could talk. Anne felt her anger begin to rise. "I knew there was something bad going on with him and Truelove and Judy kept trying to tell me it was just the flu. I've had the flu and I've seen the kids with the flu. I knew there was something wrong." Ron tried to reassure her. "I'm sure they can take care of it here. I'm just glad we got him here. That doctor didn't seem to be too upset." They exited the elevator and entered the pediatric intensive care unit waiting room.

CHAPTER 14

An elderly lady was sitting at the PICU desk. "Sign your name here so we can let you know when we have any information or if the doctor needs you."

The desk was directly on the left, inside the door. It contained a phone, the sign-in sheet and a cardboard sign that said, "Thank you for not smoking." The desk appeared as though it had been at the hospital since horse and buggy days. Someone had tried to brighten it up with a coat of paint several years ago, but that too was chipping around the edges, revealing evidence of other attempts to make the desk presentable.

There were cushioned, waiting room style chairs around the wall, and a double row of back-to-back chairs in the middle of the room. Each side of the room had a scratched and worn coffee table stacked with old magazines. The Gideons had left a Bible on each table.

In an unsuccessful attempt to make the place more cheerful, the room had been painted a dingy peach color. Anne hated peach, perhaps because she thought it clashed with her red hair. The room smelled—a combination of sweat, old coffee, stale food, smoke, and remnants of the cleanser that the janitor used yesterday to try to mask all the other odors.

In one corner, a woman was asleep on a small couch with a tattered blanket pulled over her. Anne took in the room as she looked for a seat and made her way to a chair in the corner opposite where the woman slept. The woman, asleep by herself in the corner, stirred a range of emotions in Anne. She knew that some heard good news and that some mentally and emotionally never left the waiting room.

Ron paced nervously back and forth. They pooled their change and got a diet soft drink from the machine in the waiting room and began to wait, again. They heard nothing. The woman on the couch had not moved, perhaps trying to blot out the pain of her private trauma.

After about an hour, Anne saw Dr. Kilday enter the unit.

"That was the doctor we saw earlier who just went through those doors," she informed Ron.

"Did he know what he was doing?"

Anne took a deep breath. She was glad to see Kilday. "He didn't seem to be too concerned about anything when we saw him, but he is a specialist."

Thirty minutes passed. Dr. Kilday finally appeared in the door and motioned for Anne to come out into the hallway. When Anne and Ron appeared, Dr. Kilday introduced himself to Ron.

"From the elevated temperature and the blood specimens we've taken, we feel there's a strong likelihood of infection in the shoulder area. He's quite stable now and appears to be doing rather well. We would like to perform some more studies, and take some cultures from the shoulder cavity. This would involve inserting a needle into the cavity, and I'll need to get your permission to do that."

Without hesitation, Ron spoke up. "If you feel like that's what we need to do, we don't have any problem signing whatever permission you need."

"I'll have the nurse get the release so that we can proceed as soon as we get your signature. As soon as we get it we'll go ahead."

Dr. Kilday returned to the unit and in a minute a nurse appeared with the form. Ron scanned it, signed it, and returned it to her.

Anne now had a splitting headache. She realized she hadn't had anything to eat and didn't want anything to eat. Ron did his best to cheer her up, but nothing was going to cheer her up until she knew Chad was okay.

Approximately forty-five minutes later, Dr. Wilcox reappeared. "We've taken some cultures from the shoulder cavity. That procedure went fine. We'll have those cultured in the lab to verify that there is an infection, and then after we have the scans read by the radiologist, we should have a better idea of just how extensive and widespread the infection is. At this point that's about all we can tell you."

"How's Chad doing?" Anne blurted.

Dr. Wilcox smiled. "He's resting quite comfortably. We do have him on some IVs to increase the fluid levels and actually I'm sure he's quite comfortable. He's been asleep most of the time although he roused for a few minutes. You can come back and see him, but I don't want you to stay but ten minutes."

Anne almost ran over the doctor on the way back to the unit. "Just follow me," Dr. Wilcox said with a grin, and they entered the pediatric intensive care unit.

Ron, Anne and the doctor entered the room. The wall through which they entered was made of glass from about waist high to the ceiling. The other walls appeared to be a shiny gray plastic material. Over the bed a monitor flashed signals and numbers in rhythm with Chad's heartbeat. An IV pole rose from each side of the bed, with tubes connecting the drip to Chad's arms on both sides.

Chad was lying on his back, asleep. A tube ran across his face and was attached at the nose. There was a humming noise in the background and the constant beep of the monitor. Anne stopped.

"Like I said—don't be alarmed by the—"

"What the heck is all that?" Anne whispered. She rushed to the bed and touched Chad's arm. "I knew there was more to this than—"

"It's mostly precautionary. Everybody in here gets the full treatment."

CHAPTER 15

▼

Hours passed with Anne and Ron seeing Chad for only ten minutes every two hours. They knew no more than they had already been told. It seemed like an eternity since Anne had awakened Chad that morning and hardly within her lifetime that Chad's problems had started.

From time to time she glanced outside but had no realization of the time. She noticed that it was beginning to get dark. She realized that she had been at the hospital all day and did not know anything about Chad's condition. Finally, Dr. Kilday appeared in the waiting room. Anne's body was flooded with fear.

"We've received reports on the cat scan and also from the lab on the cultures. We've verified that there is an abscess, or pocket of infection, in the shoulder area and we've started IV antibiotics. We're going to keep an eye on him all night, and we hope that we'll begin to see some improvement from the antibiotics. We're giving him a pretty substantial dose and that ought to be sufficient to see some improvement."

"What if there isn't an improvement?" Anne asked.

"We'll just have to cross that bridge when we come to it, although there are a number of procedures that we can do. However, we feel confident that this ought to do the trick. He's resting quite comfortably, and you'll be able to see him regularly, but we doubt that you'll see any visible change until tomorrow. We'll keep him closely monitored and if there is any change, the doctors can be reached quickly, and of course there will always be someone here in the ER. I can tell you that the infection is something that we'll take seriously, but at this time we don't feel that he's in any immediate danger. Any questions?"

"Okay, so this is a matter of pumping him full of antibiotics and the infection will go away and everything is going to be back to normal," thought Anne.

"So when do you think he'll be able to go home?" she asked.

Kilday allowed himself a slight smile. "If the IV antibiotics work like we think they should, we'll want to keep him here for a few days just to make sure that everything clears out, so I don't want to give you any dates, but we're feeling quite optimistic."

Dr. Kilday left and Anne and Ron were by themselves. They decided that Ron would return home to look in on Alan and the farm and relieve Anne's mother, and Anne would stay the night. She would become the lady asleep on the couch, she reflected, and she vowed that she would not leave the hospital until Chad did. At 9:00 p.m. Ron left. Anne faced the long night hours by herself. She felt the need to pray.

CHAPTER 16

▼

Anne slept fitfully throughout the night. She finally gave up before dawn. She received no word until about mid-afternoon when Dr. Kilday arrived in the waiting room. "Although it's a little early to tell, we aren't seeing the kind of progress at this point that we were hoping for."

"What can you do?"

Kilday prided himself on his ability to assuage his patients' fears. "At this point we'll just keep up the antibiotics. If things continue without any change, we may have to consider surgery. Mrs. Atkins, I know you're concerned, but I really believe that everything's going to be alright." For a moment she wished that the doctor would just put his arms around her and hold her.

"When can I go back to see him?" Anne had gone faithfully at every opportunity. As the hours passed, the nurses, becoming more familiar with her, had allowed her to stay a little longer. But she still would have preferred to stay in his room all the time.

Anne had now been at the hospital for well over twenty-four hours with nothing to eat and only diet soda in her stomach. She felt and looked horrible. The constant tension compounded everything. But she had no interest in food, rest, soap or water, at least not until Chad's condition stabilized.

Ron came in shortly after Kilday had left. She finally allowed herself to eat a little food from the cafeteria, which Ron procured, and she took a few minutes to wash up in the waiting room restroom.

On Monday evening, Dr. Kilday met with Ron and Anne in the hallway. "He's been on the antibiotics for about twenty-four hours now, and although his temperature remains basically constant, we don't feel that we're seeing much improvement. At this time, we're going to continue the antibiotics for another day unless we see some deterioration. As long as the condition seems more or less stable we would like to give the antibiotics plenty of time to work. We may also want to try some different antibiotics."

Anne's mother stayed with Alan at home that night so Ron could spend the night at the hospital with Anne. They both saw Chad throughout the night and into Tuesday in intensive care and could see no real change. He roused occasionally to talk to them and Anne felt that Chad understood where he was and what was going on. Periodic reports from the doctors verified that although Chad was remaining stable, they did not see any real improvement.

On Tuesday evening, Dr. Kilday advised that they were considering surgery. "We've tried all of the normal strategies we would try for infection. We've tried two different antibiotics, both of which should be excellent for this condition, and we've kept him pumped full of fluids. We wanted to pursue a conservative strategy as far as possible, but we feel that now we need to consider surgery."

The surgery would consist of opening the shoulder so that antibiotics could be injected directly into the joint. This would involve placing a tube into the joint. Another tube would be inserted for drainage. "We would anticipate this procedure on Wednesday morning if we don't see some real change over the night."

Ron and Anne returned to the waiting room. Anne slumped into the old couch, and Ron paced.

"Are we sure that Dr. Kilday is who we need on the case right now?" said Ron.

"The thought has crossed my mind, but I would think he would call in another specialist if he wasn't able to handle it. Apparently Dr. Truelove thought he was okay."

"I think we ought to at least mention it."

When she questioned Dr. Wilcox, Dr. Kilday came to the waiting room and assured her that this was not a complicated procedure and it did fall within his area of specialty.

They had begun to have visitors from Jasper. The majority of them were more of a hindrance than a help. Anne was glad when night came and no more visitors arrived.

Ron spent Tuesday night at the hospital with Anne. She felt that they needed to face this themselves as a family and not be bothered with explaining the situation to every curiosity seeker that came by.

On Wednesday morning, Anne's worst fears were confirmed. Chad had shown no signs of change and they wanted to do the surgery. Dr. Kilday again explained the procedure. "We plan to instill an antibiotic directly into the joint. This should get the antibiotic directly where the infection is and should give us a greater chance of clearing it out. Of course, every surgery has some risks. You realize that anytime we do surgery there is a certain risk involved, but it is my judgment that this is the best procedure to follow at this time."

Chad was scheduled for surgery at 9:00 a.m. Anne thought she might explode. She appreciated Ron's presence but felt inadequate and unable to communicate. Due to the lack of food and the excess of caffeine, she was strung out about as far as she could go. Her legs felt weak and her stomach was on fire. All she could do was wait in a semi-hypnotic trance for word from the surgery.

She tried to read but was unable to concentrate. She tried to talk with Ron but was unable to say more than a few words. Her mother arrived at 8:30 and Anne realized how much she depended on her for support even though she was now grown with her own children. She felt like a little girl who needed to be comforted by her mother.

At 10:30 a.m. Dr. Kilday signaled for them in the hallway. "The surgery went very well. We found some infectious material in the joint. We were able to clean that out and insert the tubes for instillation of the antibiotic. We've now accomplished that and we will be getting some more cultures on the material we removed from the joint. I would say that the surgery went very well and the prognosis is good. The infection was not as bad as I feared, so I would say I am cautiously optimistic."

His physician's instincts also caused him to be concerned for Anne. "I don't think the surgery could have gone any better, but we're still in a wait and see situation. I would like for you to try to rest since Chad will be in recovery for several hours and you won't be able to see him until this afternoon. By that time we ought to have some more information. I'll be glad to give you some medication to help you rest, although I suppose its asking too much for you to go home and try to get some rest there."

"No, I'm not going to be going home, and I don't need anything to help me relax."

She remained at the hospital, waiting, with virtually no news until Thursday. Early that morning, Dr. Kilday's partner, Dr. Hollings, advised her that Chad had shown signs of improvement. "It looks like the operation was successful and that we've turned the corner on the infection. I'll keep you posted throughout the day, but we're still bombarding the joint area with the antibiotic. When we performed this new procedure, we went to a different antibiotic called Strebucin, and it may be that this is what has made the difference. Sometimes it's hard to explain why one antibiotic will be better than another, but often we find that to be the case."

Chad continued to improve, although he remained on medication which kept him sleepy most of the time. By Friday, he was more alert.

Anne was concerned at his prolonged non-responsiveness. She advised Dr. Wilcox that he was always a talkative child but seemed to just look at her when she talked, even though he seemed to be more active and alert.

"He's been through a rather traumatic surgery and the disease process would also have the effect of weakening him. I'm certainly pleased to see him coming along as well as he has, but I wouldn't expect too much too quickly," Dr. Wilcox cautioned.

Anne was surprised that Dr. Kilday had not come back by the waiting room. She had not seen him since the surgery, and had communicated only with Dr. Hollings. "Probably has a busy schedule and doesn't have time to stop and chat," she decided.

On Saturday, Chad continued to show more signs of activity. He indicated that his shoulder, where the surgery had been performed, was hurting, but he remained non-communicative.

Later on Monday, Anne noticed a rather vacant stare when she talked with him. Chad had not talked to any degree since the surgery. His attempts to do so seemed strangely awkward, although she dismissed them as the result of all the medication and the surgery. Anne asked Dr. Hollings about the lack of communication and relayed to him Chad's only attempt at talking. She was surprised when Dr. Hollings uncharacteristically, though politely, cut their conversation short.

CHAPTER 17

Ron arrived at the hospital late Saturday morning. "Something's not right," Anne said. "He's getting a lot more active—I can tell he's feeling better, but he doesn't seem to want to communicate. Sometimes he just sort of looks at me. I don't know—do you think, there could be something like—maybe—brain damage?"

She discussed this with Dr. Hollings who appeared uncomfortable. He continued to assure her that everything was going to be okay.

On Saturday evening Anne collared Dr. Hollings in the hall. "There's something that's not right here. Chad still is not communicative. I think there's a possibility that there was something like—uh—brain damage or something. He seems to be getting more and more active, but he is still not talking to me. That's just not like Chad and I think you need to take a look at it."

Hollings was guarded. "We've asked a neurologist to consult with Chad and I expect that he will see him today. We certainly don't see any indication of brain damage, and I don't want you to worry about that," assured Dr. Hollings.

"This kind of thing is not at all unusual and many patients experience some disorientation after surgery. You have to remember that Chad was basically unconscious for the better part of a week and has been through a very traumatic experience. I don't want you to get alarmed, but we will have a neurologist check on him today."

Later that evening Anne was visited by the neurologist. "Ms. Atkins, I want to assure you that we find no evidence of brain damage. What I did find is that his hearing appears to be somewhat impaired. It's possible that this may be a result of the infection or the surgery."

Anne saw the reflection of her shock in the doctor's face. The blood drained from her body as if someone had pulled a giant plug in her feet.

"We're going to continue running tests to try to ascertain the extent of the situation. It's our belief that this is temporary and that it will clear up. It doesn't appear to be very severe, but this may explain to some extent Chad's inability to communicate."

In the days after surgery, Chad's ability to communicate remained constant. He tried, but it was obvious to Anne that he had difficulty hearing her or anyone else. From time to time, noises would occur in the background and Chad didn't appear to be affected by them. Anne found herself banging things, making noises in the room, or calling to Chad when he could not see her. Chad appeared to act as if everything was normal, but it was obvious to Anne that it was not.

It was Monday, and Anne and Chad were expecting to go home. They sat in silence in the hospital room. On the wall, the television was going. Hollings appeared at the door with a chart in his hand.

"So, how are we doing this morning?"

Chad sat in silence. Anne was weary. "We're ready to go home."

"Good. We think you're ready to go, too. I need to talk with you for a few minutes, though. We're going to need to give you some instructions—we're going to want Chad to continue with some therapy, and we're going to continue with some medication for a while."

Anne did not look pleased. "How long is this going to take?"

"The medication we'll keep up for a couple of weeks, at which time I want to see you in my office. We'll see about taking him off of it at that time—frankly, I would think that's likely."

"What about Dr. Kilday—We haven't seen him in ages?"

"You just happened to catch him in his rotation off—he had several days off right after Chad was admitted—and then I just followed through since we felt we were about ready to send Chad home. Does home sound like a good idea, big guy?" Hollings had turned to address Chad.

Chad gave a delayed nod of the head.

"Well, anyway, here's a card for your appointment. We've referred Chad for physical therapy—which we want him to begin as soon as possible—you'll need to call the therapist's office to set up that appointment. And we've also set you up an appointment with our speech and hearing therapist here at the hospital for next week. I talked with the therapist myself—Mr. Washington—seems like a nice guy. I think the physical therapy we can do for a few weeks, but I would say the speech will need to go on for a while."

"What about his hearing? I just don't feel good about it."

"We think that the infection had spread to his ear canals, or that possibly the medication may have had a temporary effect. At any rate, we feel like it's going to improve—that's why we're sending him to therapy—and we may want to have him followed up by a specialist—we'll just have to see. Anyway, you have a healthy normal child who may need to continue with speech and hearing therapy, but he should expect to lead a very normal life."

"What about school—I mean can he go back?"

"I believe we ought to hold off on that at least until I've seen him again. Will that be a problem?"

"We can do it, but I just hate for him to miss—my mom can watch him, and he's a good student—you know how it is."

"Yeah—I've got two of my own—but I really want him to take it easy for a while—so why don't we let him have at least a couple of weeks off."

Anne was confused. She was happy that Chad had responded to treatment and that there was no more concern about the infection.

However, she felt a great hollowness because of the hearing loss. She recognized that many people function with hearing loss, but she was uncertain as to what the future held.

CHAPTER 18

Physical therapy went well and Chad slowly regained use of his shoulder. Although weak from the illness and surgery, he seemed to regain full strength in a few weeks.

The speech and hearing therapy did not appear to go as well. Anne was frustrated by the lack of progress. She continued to be assured that Chad was making excellent progress, although Anne's informal tests at home were disturbing. Chad insisted that he could hear as well as he ever could.

Karen Holland suggested that Chad could be seen by one of the school's therapists. At least having someone else look at him to get another opinion couldn't hurt.

Anne felt that Chad was getting enough therapy as it was and didn't see the need to involve anyone else. Her thoughts changed, however, one Saturday in July.

Ron had just come in from work and Anne looked pale.

"What's the matter?"

"I'm just about sick—I don't know if I can stand this—I thought something was going to happen to Chad, and then I just don't know about his hearing. Those doctors make me so mad...."

"Why's that?"

"Chad and Alan were outside playing with firecrackers—you know those little ones we got for them? Well, I was holding the lighter and they would light one off of it and throw it. Anyway—Alan lit one and lost his hold on it and it fell right near Chad's foot. Alan yelled at Chad—but he never even turned around—and the thing went off, right by his foot, and he didn't move a muscle—never even acted like he knew it was there. Scared me to death. But he obviously couldn't hear a thing."

That evening Anne called Karen to arrange for the testing. Anne related the incident to Karen, who suggested that testing could be done at the Tennessee School for the Deaf. "I could arrange to have testing done there. Although they obviously work with deaf students, they have the equipment to detect any hearing loss. I always felt that we got the most thorough testing from them. Of course, you'll have to drive up to Knoxville and spend most of the day, but at least you'll have an independent idea of just where you stand."

The testing was scheduled for ten days away. Anne felt no great concern, but she had become more perceptive in noticing Chad's hearing limitations.

They reported to the school's administration building and were met by Will Fox, an audiologist. They went with Mr. Fox to a downstairs office and laboratory. Anne sat in an outer office and Chad went with Mr. Fox.

The testing took approximately two hours. At the conclusion, Mr. Fox invited Anne to his office at the rear of the lab, and Chad remained in one of the audiological testing areas. Anne assumed that he did not want to discuss the testing in front of Chad.

Mr. Fox showed Anne a graph revealing Chad's performance on the tests. "The numbers on the left of the graph represent decibel or dB levels, and the numbers across the top represent frequency. We tested Chad's hearing at different frequencies, that is either higher or lower pitch, and at different decibels, either higher or lower volume. If you will look on the graph, here in the 20 to 25 decibel level is where a person with average hearing will begin to perceive sounds at most frequencies, although this drops off somewhat at the higher frequencies. This range is where normal conversation occurs."

Anne saw her shock reflected in Mr. Fox's sympathetic face. He continued, although Anne heard little of what he said. "These marks on the chart show Chad's hearing level. The left ear is represented by X's and the right ear by the O's on the chart. As you can see, at the lower frequencies Chad began picking up sound in the 70 dB level with his left ear and 80 with his right and as the frequencies increased his ability to pick up sound decreased."

Anne had never seen an audiological report, but she did not need Mr. Fox to interpret the report for her. All the x and o marks on the graph were near the bottom. The marks had been traced to form a line which swerved dramatically downhill from the left. She didn't need a doctor to explain that Chad's hearing went nearly off the bottom of the graph.

"I knew he was having trouble hearing, but I thought that he was doing better. I just don't know what to think—the doctors at West Side—are you sure that this is accurate? Maybe he just didn't try because he didn't want to be bothered with this test."

"That's possible, Mrs. Atkins. We do have to make some allowance for the response of the students, although the tests have built in mechanisms for us to measure the level of effort."

Anne finally mustered enough strength to mumble, "Well, what does this mean? How serious is the loss? I mean, I know it's going to get better, but what does this mean right now?"

"Of course I'm not qualified as a physician to tell you what this means for the future, but according to state guidelines, this would be considered a profound hearing loss."

Mr. Fox couldn't find the strength to tell Anne what he was thinking. According to state educational regulations, Chad was profoundly deaf.

Will Fox had seen hundreds of children with deafness, and he had not seen any with this degree of hearing loss that made any significant recovery. Tennessee School for the Deaf was full of students who had better hearing capability than Chad.

CHAPTER 19

Anne had to talk to somebody. She finally got Karen. "So, what did you find out?"

"I would say the test results were not very good. I really don't know what to believe. According to Dr. Hollings, Chad has lost some of his hearing but should be getting better. According to the tests at Knoxville, he's virtually deaf. I don't know where to turn."

"I know its confusing. Since Dr. Hollings and his group have been on the case longer, maybe they have a better understanding of the situation."

"Dr. Hollings wasn't the one who started with Chad, it was Dr. Kilday. I don't know what happened to him. He seems to have just disappeared. Sometimes I think they're just trying to make it look better, just to cover themselves."

"I think you ought to do whatever is necessary to satisfy yourself. How can you know what to do unless you know the truth?"

"I'm not sure any more if you can know what the real situation is. It seems like you only get a piece of the truth here and there. Sometimes things aren't what they appear to be—you know what I mean?"

"If I were you, I'd try to get him to the best doctor I could find, and have him tested. Surely, they can give you an accurate idea of how well he can hear."

"Where am I going to get that kind of information? I mean they don't just advertise in the phone book."

"Maybe they could help at the school for the deaf, or maybe Dr. George would know."

It took a week, but Dr. Truelove's office provided the names of physicians at the University of Virginia, Duke University and the University of South Carolina. Anne called all three facilities and received the best reception at the University of South Carolina. However, she was advised that she would need a referral from a physician before Chad could be seen there. Anne called Dr. Truelove's office and Judy agreed to call the University of South Carolina to make the referral.

An appointment was scheduled for approximately two weeks away. Having grown wiser, Ron and Anne dreaded the trip, but felt they needed to do everything to pursue possible treatment.

Even forewarned, Ron and Anne had not envisioned the battery of tests Chad underwent at the South Carolina Eye and Ear Institute. They met Dr. James Brice at the Institute and spent all day Wednesday and half of Thursday there.

Dr. Brice's summary at the end of the two days was short and basically reinforced the information they had received earlier at the school for the deaf. Dr. Brice was noncommittal on the possibilities of improvement. He reiterated what they already knew, suggested a course of therapy similar to what Chad was already receiving, and left little hope for the future. He declined to express an opinion as to the cause of Chad's hearing loss.

It was at this point that Maurice Washington, the therapist at West Side, approached Anne about the possibility that something had gone wrong.

CHAPTER 20

▼

After some prodding from Johnny, Anne finally called Sam Trestle's office. "I believe Johnny talked with you about my case. I'm really just interested in getting some more information."

Sam had talked with hundreds of clients. *She doesn't want to get my hopes up or commit herself to letting me represent her,* he realized.

"Why don't you come in and we can talk some more about your case. I can give you some preliminary information and then we can see where we can go from there. These suits need to be filed within a year, and there usually is a lot of work that needs to be done before they're filed. So, I think it would be very much to your advantage to get in here and get things started, even if that means just beginning to collect some information so you can make a decision as to what you want to do. Time is very much of the essence."

Sam didn't want to say that he wanted her to get in as quickly as possible so that another attorney wouldn't have an opportunity to steal the case, but that was in his mind. What he had told Anne wasn't incorrect either, but he remembered Johnny's advice that he shouldn't appear overly anxious.

"I could probably come in this afternoon if you have some time on your calendar or tomorrow afternoon after work, either day."

Sam's heart leaped. "Heck yes, I can see you any time and if I have to cancel something else to work it out, I will," he thought. However, he told Anne, "Let me check my calendar and check with Alma, but I think we can probably find some time this afternoon." Sam removed his small appointment book from his coat pocket. He had nothing on his calendar for that day and only one brief appointment for tomorrow.

"Looking at my calendar it would be better for me to see you this afternoon. My schedule looks a little more crowded tomorrow," Sam responded.

"What time?" Anne asked.

Sam paused again, looked at his appointment book and tried to guess what time Anne got off from work. He suspected it would be either 4:00 or 5:00. He thought it best not to suggest 5:00 since Anne would ascertain that he had set the time specifically for her, and again he didn't want to appear overly anxious. "I would think about 4:30 would be best for me if you can work that out," he finally responded.

"That would be fine with me, I get off at 4:30 and I can be there pretty quickly. Would it matter if I'm a few minutes late?" Anne asked.

"That'll be fine. It'll give me time to get everything wrapped up so that we should be able to spend some uninterrupted time talking about your case. We usually close about 5:00 anyway, and I could stay a little late today. I would suspect we'll need more than thirty minutes or so, but I'm used to staying late to work around people's work schedules. You know where my office is and I'll see you as soon as possible after work today."

Sam was elated. He wanted to spend a few minutes in the books so he could talk more intelligently with Anne when she came in, but he could hardly contain his excitement. He even called Lynn at school and left a message for her to call when she had a chance.

Anne was excited but guarded. She still didn't know how she felt about Sam Trestle. She had no reason to have optimism over Chad's condition and the only avenue of hope she could see was the potential for seeking justice, or revenge, from Dr. Kilday.

Anne had known Sam since grade school. Everybody pretty much knew everyone else in Jasper, even though Sam had been a few years ahead of Anne in school. At one time she remembered thinking Sam was cute, but the age difference had kept them from getting to know one another very well.

Anne called Ron at work to tell him she had made the appointment and to see if he wanted to go. He felt that it would be best for him to go along. Anne suspected that he would and knew that he could get off work early if needed.

Ron was still in a cautious mode. "Now, I don't want you to go getting all excited. I know nothing is going to satisfy you until you've talked to a lawyer, but we just don't need to get excited about this lawsuit thing."

Ron's reluctance just excited Anne more. She had decided she was going to see that a lawsuit was filed no matter what she had to do. Based on the advertisements she had seen in the Chattanooga newspapers and on the Chattanooga television stations, she felt sure that she could find a lawyer somewhere who would file the case and she intended to find that person and see that suit was filed if it bankrupted them.

Sam spent about an hour looking at statutes and court rules to familiarize himself with some of the details that he thought would be involved in his conversation with Anne and Ron that afternoon. He knew it was important to make a good impression, to appear confident, experienced, and informed. He even went home at lunch to put on his best suit.

Anne arrived at Sam's office at 4:30 p.m. She had left work a few minutes early and rushed. Ron, not wanting to appear too anxious, arrived about five minutes later. Both were nervous.

Alma advised Sam by the intercom that both had arrived, although Sam was completely aware of their arrival and everything they had said and done since they entered the office. His office was only a few steps away from Alma's desk and the waiting room and the door were casually left open. He paused a minute to attempt making some order of his desk and walked to the waiting room.

"Hi Anne-Marie, it's good to see you again," Sam shook Anne's hand and then turned to Ron. "Hi Ron, I appreciate y'all coming in. I'm sorry it's under these circumstances, but I feel that you've done the right thing to put your mind at ease and get some more information." Sam turned and motioned for Ron and Anne to follow him back to his office.

"Its good to see you all again. I don't guess we've seen that much of each other since school, except in passing."

Ron seemed eager to renew his acquaintance with Sam. "I guess I was a few years behind you in school, and I remember when I was playing baseball over at the elementary school for the eighth grade team, and you and some of the players from the high school came over to work with us. I thought that was the greatest thing in the world."

"Yeah, I thought it was fun, too, and it wasn't too long after that that I blew out my knee."

"Did you ever play much after that?"

"Never played again for the high school. I was only a junior, and never got to play more than a few innings in a varsity game."

Anne had been sitting quietly, but realized the meeting could last forever if Ron got started talking sports. "I was remembering you and Lynn from school after I talked with Johnny the other night. I remember when she was homecoming queen. How did the two of you ever get together?"

"Heck if I know. For some reason, she seemed to discover that I was alive in our senior year, and I guess we've more or less been together ever since."

Sam knew it was time to get down to business. "I really do appreciate you all coming in. If there's a way I can help out, I'll be glad to."

"In my brief conversation with Johnny, and then later with Anne, I have an idea of what you're here for, but I think it'd be better for you to just tell me what's going on. Then I'll try to give you some of my preliminary thoughts after I've heard all your story."

"Why don't you go ahead and just tell him the whole story Anne; I think you know more of the details," Ron volunteered, knowing that it would go far better if Anne told the story, and as a practical matter, that she was either going to tell the story herself or die.

"What is the extent of the hearing loss, or do you know?" Sam asked. What he was actually thinking about was the damages he could ask for. Better to settle first things first.

"That's an interesting question," Anne said. "Some of the tests indicate what is known as a profound hearing loss. The doctors at West Side feel like it's not that serious and that he is improving all along and that there should be further improvement to the extent that he should eventually just be hard of hearing. Some of the other doctors we have taken him to, including this one specialist, are not as optimistic."

Sam mentally compared the level of the damages with other cases he had handled and concluded that it would not be as great as a loss of a limb or severe impairment to other bodily functions. If Chad was basically okay but just couldn't hear as well, that would certainly be the kind of thing for which he could recover damages; however, Sam concluded that the child was okay and would just have the annoyance of not being able to hear very well. The wheels in his head were turning. Of course, it would make it difficult for him to pursue certain types of employment, but still he had his mind. He could read, write, and work. Apparently there was not a lot of pain involved and, of course, pain and suffering would constitute much of the damage.

After Anne had related the story, Ron added, "This Dr. Kilday seems to have been hiding something. Neither of us has ever liked him. I would think that if we could get him in front of a Marion County jury that they wouldn't like him either."

Sam wasn't sure whether to inform Ron and Anne that if Dr. Kilday was the only defendant, the case would have to be filed in Chattanooga. First, he didn't want to be overly problematic, and second he worried that this might give them more reason to want to hire a Chattanooga attorney. "Who do you suspect may be responsible for malpractice, assuming that we can prove any of the doctors was negligent?"

"I've thought about that a lot, and I've looked at the medical records. Dr. Kilday was responsible for Chad at the hospital, until Dr. Hollings took over. And Dr. Wilcox was also involved."

"Do you think there's a possibility that someone on the hospital staff, other than a doctor, may have done something wrong?" Sam was asking questions to keep Ron and Anne talking, to appear intelligent and to get as much information as possible. However, he knew that the answers to these questions would have to be determined by medical experts after extensive research of the records.

"We really don't have any information other than what Maurice Washington told me," Anne said. "Do you think that means anything in our situation?"

Sam thought he needed to do some advising. He had learned that clients wanted his evaluation of the situation, even if many times it meant just advising them of the obvious. "In my experience it's not all that unusual for the hospital staff to realize that something has happened. They may very well know exactly what happened, or they may just have a suspicion that something has happened. However, the hospital staff, therapists, and nurses are like everybody else. There's a rumor mill or grapevine there and it probably won't be very long before most of the staff knows something happened. Of course, we need to be alert to the possibility that this fellow is just trying to help out his lawyer buddy and that he does what he can to round up cases, and it may not have any great significance at all. But, at this point, I would treat it as credible."

Sam talked with Anne and Ron for another hour, explaining some of the basics of a medical negligence or malpractice suit. He tried not to burden them with problems or details.

"The primary thing that we're going to be interested in is finding a doctor who can talk with you, review all of the medical records from the hospital, and give us an opinion as to whether there is negligence involved."

"In cases like this, it's necessary to prove that the physician was negligent, that the patient was damaged in some way, and that the physician's negligence was the cause of the patient's damage. It is also necessary to prove that it was foreseeable that the action of the physician, that is his negligence, would have caused the damage. If we can't prove one or more of these elements of the case, then we can't recover. Actually most of the legal principles are the same in all negligence cases. I have the case where the woman fell and hit her head and died over at the shopping center. Although it's called a wrongful death case, we still have to show negligence and causation and damages."

"In a medical malpractice case, we generally prove the negligence of the physician by showing that he violated the standard of care for physicians in that specialty. It's also necessary to show what the standard of care is among physicians in Chattanooga. We can do this by bringing in a physician from somewhere else; however, they would need to be familiar with the standard of care in geographical areas the size of Chattanooga. For example, the standard of care in Washington, D.C. is not necessarily the same as the standard of care in Jasper. So, our medical expert is not only going to need to be familiar with the medical aspects of the case but also familiar with the standard of care in the Chattanooga area."

"As you know, it's usually difficult to find a doctor who will testify. Additionally, we not only have to find a doctor, but we have to find an orthopedic specialist familiar with the standard of care in Chattanooga.

I would be surprised if there's an orthopedic specialist in Chattanooga who will testify against Dr. Kilday."

"Likewise, if we include other doctors, we may have to find experts in their specialties. In my experience most medical negligence cases are won or lost on the testimony of the experts. The big problem is that it's an unusual physician who has the inclination to testify against a colleague."

Sam got Ron and Anne to sign a medical release so he could obtain the medical records. "This wouldn't commit us to filing suit, but it will let me find a medical expert to look at the records. We need to have someone lined up who can tell us there was negligence before we file suit, and if we're going to do that we really need to get moving. Likewise, in order to be able to pay the doctor, to cover the expenses of getting the records and mailing them, I would like to get a retainer just to cover expenses."

Sam hated to discuss fees; he could feel the nervousness, particularly in Ron's countenance. "I would suggest one thousand dollars. Frankly, this won't cover the cost of the doctor, but it should cover the cost of all the records, my long distance calls, possibly some travel to try to line up a doctor, and perhaps enough to pay him to get him started looking at the records. I won't obligate us to pay anything to the doctor without talking to you. Regardless of what decision you make about filing suit or any other decisions, I feel like you need to get started, if nothing else to satisfy your minds that you've pursued every possibility."

Ron did not like the idea of paying a thousand dollars. Now that money was brought up neither did Anne, but she agreed, adding, "Can we get you a check tomorrow? We'll need to talk about where we're going to get the money."

Anne had no doubt that she was pursuing this matter to conclusion. She realized that she was going to have to spend some money along the way, and she felt that getting all of the records and getting them to a doctor who could review them was a reasonable expenditure.

"Oh, by the way, we may be able to use Dr. Brice as a witness. He's the specialist who saw Chad. He's been cooperative when I've asked him questions—I sensed that he was guarded, but I feel like he's honest and he likes Chad."

"Well, I wouldn't want to get our hopes up because as I told you it's a very unusual doctor that would want to testify. However, we can certainly give him a try. Where is he located?"

"He's at the South Carolina Eye and Ear Institute in Columbia."

CHAPTER 21

▼

Gloria Sharp sat at a small desk in the outer waiting room of the medical records office at West Side Hospital going through the day's incoming mail. Among the large stack of envelopes that had come in over the weekend was one from Samuel D. Trestle, Attorney at Law, Jasper, Tennessee. She opened it, along with the others, and found a letter from the attorney, enclosing a medical release form signed by Anne Atkins and requesting the medical records of Chad Atkins. She laid the documents in a stack along with others received in the morning's mail.

Each request for records was processed individually. Requests from physicians or hospital personnel were processed first. Requests from insurance companies were processed second. Most days found several requests from attorneys, which went to the bottom of the stack.

Gloria also had a list of files which had been "red-flagged," usually by the attending physician. This meant that the doctor wished to be alerted if a request for medical records came in.

Gloria took the various requests to the individuals responsible for responding to them and returned to her desk. She dialed the office of West Side Orthopedics Associates. "This is Gloria at Medical Records. Would you tell Dr. Kilday that we've had a request for medical records on Chad Atkins?"

"I'm sorry but Dr. Kilday is in surgery right now," responded the voice at the other end. "Sheesh," thought Gloria. "I don't care where he is, I just need to get the message to him." However, she responded, "Could you please see that Dr. Kilday gets the message? He red-flagged that file."

"Okay, I'll see that he gets the message when he comes in, but I'm not sure when he can return your call. He's very busy today."

"Thank you," said Gloria and she hung up. She wondered where the doctors' offices got some of the dimwits that answered their phones. She had no doubt that Dr. Kilday was busy and she didn't really care where he was or whether he got the message. She put a red check mark beside Chad Atkins' name on her list and went on about her duties.

At 10:30 Dr. Kilday called. "Please pull the Chad Atkins file and hold it for me. I'll be down to look it over this afternoon. Also, I'd like for you to put a hold on that file. I don't want it to go out until I tell you."

"Hospital policy requires that all information requests be answered within two days," responded Gloria in her most snippy voice.

"I don't care what hospital policy is. I want you to hold the file until I tell you to let it go. I'll be down to look at it when I get time." Dr. Kilday hung up the phone. He wondered where the hospital got some of the dimwits who answered their phones.

Gloria made a mental note to process the request for information by the end of the second day. At 1:00 p.m., Dr. Kilday came to the medical records office. "I'm Dr. Kilday, I'd like to see the Chad Atkins' records."

Gloria got up from her desk and went through the door into the medical records room. She stopped to chat with some of the other workers in the office, got herself a cup of coffee and reappeared with the records.

Dr. Kilday took note of the cup of coffee. "When doctors need records, they need them as quickly as possible. I don't have time to stand around waiting while you're drinking coffee. Where can I go to look at these records?" Gloria directed him to a table in the medical records office.

"I need to have some privacy going over these records, is there not an office I can use?"

Gloria took him to the supervisor's office and directed the request to her. As she left, she noticed that the two lingered for a few minutes and then the supervisor left her office and closed the door leaving Jack Kilday to review the records in her office. She rolled her eyes toward Gloria as she made her way back into the file room.

Jack Kilday remained in the office for over an hour. As he left he told Gloria, "I've left the records file on the desk. I'll be back in an hour to finish reviewing the files. I want the records left on the desk and undisturbed." Not waiting for a reply, he exited the office.

At 3:00 p.m. that afternoon Dr. Kilday returned with a briefcase. He remained in the supervisor's office for approximately fifteen minutes, leaving without saying anything.

At 4:00 p.m., a neatly groomed young man in a pin-striped suit appeared. Gloria recognized him as one of the hospital's attorneys.

"This must be a rather interesting case," she thought. The young man introduced himself, made his way to the supervisor's office and was still going through the records when Gloria left.

The next morning, she found the records on her desk with a note from the attorney to forward copies to Samuel D. Trestle, Attorney at Law.

CHAPTER 22

▼

Sam received the records in the mail the next day. He was particularly pleased with the promptness and condition of the records. Sometimes through the copying process, the records were scarcely legible. His experience with West Side had generally been better than with some of the other medical records offices.

He dictated a letter to Dr. Brice at the South Carolina Eye and Ear Institute, enclosing copies of the medical records. Sam had reviewed scores of medical records and found nothing particularly unusual among these.

He also called Dr. Cliff Hixson, his own family physician in Jasper. Cliff had been a high school classmate and Sam often picked his mind for helpful medical information.

"What can I do for you today, Sam my good man?" responded Dr. Hixson. "Do you have a cold or some other treacherous malady, or are you just looking for some free medical advice?"

"I suppose this falls into the latter category," responded Sam, "I'm sorry for the sake of your pocketbook that I'm in basically good health right now, but I do need a little bit of input if you can help me out."

"Okay, I'll give it a try. What's the situation?" Sam gave the highlights of Chad's medical treatments to Dr. Hixson.

"There's not anything that strikes me as being wrong on the part of the physician, I'm sorry to say for your case. Sounds like to me that you might question whether the infection was treated soon enough, and I suppose it's possible that, had it been treated sooner, the infection would not have spread to the ear area. However, from what you've told me, it sounds like procedure was followed appropriately, and I would have a hard time criticizing the time frames. I'd have probably done the same thing if he had come to my office. By the way, Dr. Truelove did mention the situation to me and I think he was a little bit nervous. Just thought I'd let you know that."

"It sure would cause me a problem if I had to file suit against Dr. Truelove, and actually we're sort of centering in on Dr. Jack Kilday over in Chattanooga. Do you know what kind of a reputation he has?"

"He has a first rate reputation, and the group he's with does also. I don't know him very well, but I would have to say that he's not one of the warmest people I've ever met. You need to know that impression has only come from a couple of instances where I was introduced to him."

"That's the impression I get from the Atkins, too. I suppose we can't sue somebody for not being very warm. Do you have any other suggestions of anybody I might talk with?"

"Has the family seen any other specialists relating to the hearing condition? I think I would try to run it by them first. They might be able to give you some information. I would have to say that it does look strange that the kid was apparently healthy when he went into the hospital and then came out with this loss of hearing, but I can't think of anything to explain it other than the spreading of the infection. The only other suggestion I would have is that you send the records to some docs in other specialties. Someone may pick up on something that could be significant, although I really don't know what it would be."

Sam was somewhat dejected after his phone call with Dr. Hixson. Although he maintained a general family practice, he usually had enough knowledge and interest to pick up any obvious points. The fact that there were apparently no obvious points simply meant that, if they could find any angle upon which to file suit, the negligence claim would not be very obvious to the jury.

Other pressing business kept Sam occupied for the next several days. He continued to think about the case during slack times, such as driving back and forth to work, and sometimes found himself thinking about the case at home. Sam often mused that this was when he did his best work, almost absentmindedly turning the facts of his cases over and over in his mind, trying to find the best approach. Nothing came to him this time.

He was surprised to receive a prompt response from the South Carolina Eye and Ear Institute. He was even more surprised to find that Dr. Brice, rather than writing, had asked him to call so that they could discuss the case over the phone.

CHAPTER 23

▼

"Hello"

"It's me—did you get the records?"

"Sure—no problem. It's like I told you. Nobody pays that much attention. What should I do with them?"

"Just keep them at your house. I don't think I'd keep them at the office."

"You sure you don't want me to just destroy them?"

"No—not now."

"Why not—I just don't like having these things laying around."

"Don't leave them laying around—for goodness sake, put them where nobody's gonna find them."

"I think we ought to just burn 'em—that way we'll know nobody's gonna find them."

"Look. Don't ask so many questions. The less you know, the better at this point. Besides, I'm not sure we won't need them to reappear somewhere along the line."

"How's that gonna happen?"

"I don't know—hopefully we won't need them—I just want to keep our options open."

"What if somebody finds them—won't we be in a lot of trouble?"

"How could anybody find them? Hide them some place at your house where nobody is going to find them."

"Can't the police come search my house or something?"

"No. That's just in criminal cases. I'm talking about really hiding them. I don't mean put them in your desk or something. Can't you put them under a board in the attic—something like that."

"Okay. Nobody's going to find them. Are we going to be in serious trouble?"

"Not if nobody finds those things. I just think this is our best shot— we'll let it go along for a while and see what happens. I think it's gonna work just the way I planned."

"Okay. I'm gonna trust you with this—but it better not backfire."

"Don't worry."

Chapter 24

"Hi, Anne, this is Sam Trestle. I just wanted to let you know that I got a short letter from Dr. Brice over at the University of South Carolina."

"Yeah—what did he have to say?"

"He really didn't have anything to say. He wants me to give him a call."

"You don't know why he wants you to call?"

"No, I thought you might have an idea. Usually these guys just write a letter, if you can get them to do anything at all."

"Probably wants to tell us to leave him alone."

"Maybe so, but I would normally take it as a good sign that I can talk to him, rather than just get it off a piece of paper."

"The way my luck's going lately, I doubt it."

"Things not going too well?"

"Don't get me started. Words can't describe it. Chad's not doing anything in school, and he seems to be losing touch with his old friends. All the school wants to do is stick him into some special class. He tried out for the little league all-star team and didn't make it—would you like me to go on? I'm sorry, sometimes I just get carried away. Anyway, things aren't going very well."

"I'm sorry. Guess there's not much I can do about those things, but I'll do my best on this end."

"I don't expect you to do anything about all those other things—I just get carried away—I really don't have anybody to talk to—people don't know how to relate to Chad, or me either, I guess. But I feel like we're becoming a bunch of hermits out here."

"Maybe when I talk to Dr. Brice we'll have some good news."

"If it's bad news just don't call."

Sam started to hang up and had another thought. "Have you talked to Dr. Truelove lately?"

"No—more of the same. I think he may know somehow that we've been talking to you. The last time I called over there, Judy seemed real strange. Normally we'd see him at church, but since all this came up, we haven't been going very regularly—I'm not sure we're his favorite people right now."

"Okay—I'll let you know what I find out."

Anne did not tell Sam that part of her problem was her concern about him. Sam seemed to be moving slowly. Sometimes she wished she had talked with an attorney at one of the larger firms in Chattanooga. Anne's impression of Sam was that he did things in his own good time when he got around to them. She comforted herself by remembering that she and Ron had agreed to hire Sam only for the purpose of getting the medical records and making an initial evaluation of the case. If things didn't begin to move before long, they always had the option of consulting another attorney.

Anne didn't know who the lawyer was going to be, for sure, but she knew who the object of the case was going to be. Anne remembered where she was sitting when she realized something was going on and Kilday was responsible for it. Chad had been transferred to Pediatric Intensive Care. Ron and Anne had taken up residence in the PICU waiting room.

Time stood still. Mornings and nights had no significance and the only events that marked the day were the short visits every two hours.

In between those times, Anne slept, paced, read and just thought. It was during one of those times that she realized Kilday had done something.

She thought back to the first time she had met him. Charming, professional—she had trusted him. She found herself attracted to him. She had silently kicked herself when he had put his hand on her shoulder and she had felt herself blush; liking his touch and attention. One of the downsides to her red hair and light complexion.

He had been right there when Chad was admitted. Everything was going to be all right.

Then he had just disappeared. Not a word, not an explanation—he just never showed up again.

And Anne had been sitting in PICU. Worrying, thinking everything over and it suddenly dawned on her. What happened to Dr. Kilday?

Wouldn't somebody have just said something if there was another explanation? Something had gone wrong with Chad—she hadn't known exactly what—and Kilday had vanished.

Later, in the hospital library, she had run into him. He'd just turned and left. Not a word, not a nod—nothing.

And now she hated him. She hated Hollings. She hated the group. At least they could have told her. "Something's gone wrong. Chad has lost his hearing and Dr. Kilday has screwed up." Then she could have dealt with it.

As it was, she knew—but she didn't know. She knew what had happened, the final result. She knew who. But she didn't know why. She also knew that Kilday was going to pay.

CHAPTER 25

Sam sat in one of the pew-like benches in the courtroom in the Jasper County Courthouse. He had loosened his tie and was trying to relax while talking with his clients, a son and two daughters of the woman who had died in the shopping center accident. The case had been tried for two days, much to the displeasure of Judge Richard Higgins, who felt that the facts of any situation known to man could be presented to a jury in one day. Sam felt that the Judge's impatience had cost him some of the opportunity to present his case. Nonetheless, his case had been solid and he was expecting a sizeable verdict for his clients.

He was exhausted, yet excited by the possibility of the verdict he hoped would be soon forthcoming. He had finished his argument to the jury less than an hour ago. It had gone just as he had planned, meticulously over months of preparation.

Sam had thousands of his own dollars invested in the case, advancing money for court costs, depositions and other expenses, not to mention the hundreds of hours he had invested in the case. Now it was all going to be worth it. He had a relaxed, easy smile as he conversed with his clients.

The jury had been out for approximately thirty minutes. He didn't expect them to be out for too long, but if they were discussing the kind of damages he hoped for, he knew that it would take a while. Although it was approaching 5:00, he suspected that Judge Higgins would make the jury keep deliberating on into the night. Sam knew that possibility had a downside; however, he felt that generally it favored him since the passion and emotion of the trial were still fresh on their minds.

Sam wandered outside the courtroom and into the clerk's office to chat with some of the women who were closing the office for the day. Just then, Wallace, the deputy assigned to serve as court bailiff, opened the door which led from the courtroom to the clerk's office, looked at Sam with a raised eyebrow and said, "Jury's back."

Sam's heart skipped a beat, sunk for a second and then began racing. It was too early for the jury to be back. If they were back this quickly, they wouldn't have had time to discuss the issue of damages. It was generally thought that if the jury came back quickly, it was a good sign for the defense.

Surely that couldn't be the case. "I guess this shows that all the old lawyer maxims about juries can't be believed," Sam thought as he hustled into the courtroom.

He was almost afraid to look at his clients since he knew they were probably thinking the same thing. "Better to keep a confident air," he thought as he found his way to the counsel table.

With everyone standing in place, Wallace brought the jury in. They had a somewhat casual look on their faces as Wallace led them in to face the Judge in semi-circle fashion in front of his bench.

Judge Higgins looked over his glasses at the jury. "Have you reached a verdict?"

"Yes, Your Honor, we have," said the foreman, a tall red and gray-haired ex-military man who reminded Sam of one of the older lawyers in town. Sam had only allowed this man to be on the jury because his clients liked him and once again Sam wished that he had excused him with one of the challenges he had at the beginning of the trial.

"And what is your verdict," boomed Judge Higgins from the bench.

Sam snapped back to attention as he realized he had become lost in thought over the selection of the jury foreman. He reassured himself, put on his cautious grin and gave attention to the jury's spokesman.

"We find in favor of the defendants, Your Honor."

Sam had not led a life without disappointment. Particularly in a small town law practice, you take your clients as you find them, sometimes having to represent the client on the worst end of the deal.

However, nothing he had experienced in life to this point prepared him for the shock and the disappointment of this jury's decision. Sam felt his knees go weak and sweat on his forehead. In an instant, he knew that he had taken a severe financial blow, and that there was nothing he could do about it. He could file appeals until the end of time, but this jury's verdict was going to stand. He needed to say something to his clients, but words failed him.

The defendants were congratulating themselves at the other table. He knew that the defense attorney was going to walk over and shake his hand and he tried to prepare himself for it. Sure enough, he saw him coming, braced himself and stuck out his hand. Thus aroused from his shock, he returned to his clients to see them in stunned disbelief. He breathed a sigh of relief as he remembered that it was the clients who were steadfast in turning down an offer of $100,000.00 to settle the case. An offer that Sam and the clients felt was far short of a fair settlement. Now the knowledge that he could have one-third of that amount in his bank account gnawed at him.

He walked out of the courthouse with his clients, promised to give them a call tomorrow and stumbled aimlessly, virtually unconsciously to his car and drove home. He didn't want to face Lynn with his failure. He simply wanted to go home, crawl into bed and sleep for a couple of weeks. A luxury he knew that he didn't have due to the pressing needs of the Atkins case.

The Atkins case. Now he had to go through the whole process again with the potential of the same bitter, disappointing result. All of a sudden he wished that he hadn't taken on the additional responsibility for the Atkins. He didn't know if he could emotionally bring himself to go through that process again.

CHAPTER 26

"This is Sam Trestle in Jasper, Tennessee, calling for Dr. Brice." Sam avoided the use of the term "attorney," having found long ago that many people, particularly physicians, did not accept his call for that reason alone.

The feminine voice on the other end of the line, after a minute long absence, announced that Dr. Brice was with a patient, but that he would return the call. Sam left his number and hung up.

To Sam's surprise, within thirty minutes Dr. Brice returned the call. "Dr. Brice, I received your letter several days ago, and I apologize for not getting to you sooner."

"That's quite all right. I'm never in a hurry to talk to you attorney-types."

"I'm sorry to bother you, and I know that you're busy, but I really would appreciate any information you could give me on the Chad Atkins situation."

"The reason that I wanted to call you, and I might add that I very seldom do this, but I wanted to discuss something with you, that I really didn't want to put in writing."

Sam's antenna went up.

"In reviewing the record, it seems to me that the normal conclusion would be that unfortunately the infection simply spread, lodged in the ear canal, and caused quite a bit of damage to this child's hearing mechanism. I know you're looking for evidence of negligence, and I suppose we might speculate on whether if he had received appropriate attention sooner this might not have happened."

"However, I wouldn't be able to help you by telling you that I think the doctor should have taken action sooner, and I certainly wouldn't be able to tell you that this might not have happened even if he had hospitalized him the first day he saw him. It's very possible that the infection was already in the ear canal. So, I'm afraid as far as I'm concerned you'd be barking up the wrong tree on negligence from that standpoint."

Sam noted the qualification which Dr. Brice added.

"On the other hand, if I were researching this situation, and had access to all of the information that I wanted, I think I might pursue the use of Strebucin. This is a medication, that if taken in large amounts, can cause deafness."

"We rarely find any cases of that, however, because this is a well known side effect, and it's relatively easy to monitor the amounts that are being given. This is a perfectly good medication, but it does require monitoring in order not to over-medicate. If the patient is over medicated, deafness can result. As I say, this is highly unusual. In fact I've never seen a patient who became deaf because of the use of this medication, but it could happen."

"So I wouldn't be able to advise you that this is what caused the problem. Nevertheless, it would be something that I would want to rule out." Dr. Brice kept going and Sam was writing feverishly.

"One other thing makes me think that this is a possibility. There doesn't seem to be any indication from the chart of any discomfort in the ear region. If the patient had enough infection in the ear canals to cause the kind of damage that he apparently received, there should have been discomfort. Also, the fact that both canals were involved would seem to me to point to the medication, as opposed to infection. Here again, it's entirely possible, although not as likely, that the infection could have spread to both ears."

Sam was trying to digest all of this. He continued to write in silence when the doctor quit speaking. Dr. Brice brought him back to reality by asking him if this was all clear.

"I think I understand generally what you are saying, and I'm just trying to make a few notes. How could we ascertain whether he received too much medication?"

"Congratulations, you've hit on the key question to the whole puzzle. Normally a doctor would take blood samples. If the levels begin to get higher than they should be, then the dosage would be cut back before any harm was done, and this should be sufficient to avoid any damage. In the records, there are orders for blood monitoring, however, there appears to be no record of samples. Why that is, I don't know. It's possible that we just don't have all the records, and that there were samples taken of which we do not have copies. It's also possible that sampling was discontinued."

"So what does the fact that these records are missing mean to you?"

"I don't know—it certainly throws an interesting light on things."

"Yes, it does," said Sam, deep in thought.

He still had one major hurdle. Under Tennessee law, a physician may not testify in a medical negligence unless he practices in a state which borders Tennessee. Since South Carolina missed by several miles, he had to locate a medical expert willing to testify who did reside in a state that bordered Tennessee.

"Uh, Doctor, do you know any physicians who might be able to review this with me and work with me on it who live in Tennessee, or one of its border states? Unfortunately, since you reside in South Carolina you wouldn't be able to testify."

"I can't tell you how disappointed I am," cracked Dr. Brice. "If you'll give me a few days, I'll try to put together a list of people that you might contact and mail it out to you. Other than that, I don't know what help

I've been or whether I can give you any more help or not. You need to keep in mind that all these things I've told you are merely speculations."

"Thanks doctor. I believe you've confirmed what I was thinking. Seems like we're headed in the right direction."

CHAPTER 27

He picked up the phone again to call Anne. At least he had good news to report, from that standpoint.

"So, can we use him as a witness at the trial?"

Sam had been afraid she was going to ask. "Unfortunately, no. Any medical expert has to practice in a state that borders Tennessee."

"You're kidding."

"Afraid not. So, although I've got some good information, I still don't have a live witness. Also, some of the records appear to be missing from the files."

"Hmmm. What do you think about that?"

"Don't exactly know at this point—but it might be helpful."

"Uh—Did you know I went over and looked at the records—I hope that doesn't make a difference."

"I can't imagine that it would. I mean, why would you take a record out of the file?"

"Yeah. That's what I was thinking. Why would anyone accuse me?"

Time was growing short. Sam had only ten days to file suit before the statute of limitations ran out on the case. He needed medical documentation before filing suit. He was beginning to feel panicky. Sometimes, at times like these, Sam wondered why he became involved in these high-pressure situations.

"I've exhausted our list of possible doctor witnesses and still haven't found a thing. I'm going to keep trying, but it looks like I'm back to starting from scratch."

Anne again wondered why she had not gone to one of the larger firms in Chattanooga. Surely they would have better contacts than Sam. Anne thought back to her previous conversation and the help she had gotten from the Tennessee School for the Deaf.

"The only other idea I have is that you talk with the Tennessee School for the Deaf in Knoxville. They may know some doctors and might be able to give you some leads."

"I'll give them a call and see if they have any possibilities." Sam made an appointment with Anne and Ron for that afternoon to discuss the entire situation, hung up the phone, and asked Alma to get the telephone number at TSD.

He had spent hours trying to get in touch with the doctors with whom he had already discussed the case. It was always tough trying to get through to any of the doctors. Only one had returned his telephone call. The rest he had simply continued to bother until he finally got through. He called TSD and got the name of two doctors in the Knoxville area who had seen some of the deaf students at TSD. Sam hung up and began the calling process.

As Sam knew it would, the Atkins' case was taking so much of his time that he was neglecting his other work. This had a two-fold consequence. First, he was beginning to sense that other clients were becoming dissatisfied with progress on their cases. Second, since the Atkins' case was producing no income, and he was not generating income from other cases, he was beginning to feel the financial pinch. However, he had no choice other than to put everything aside to lay the groundwork for filing the Atkins' case.

Sam felt that it was necessary to get a doctor's opinion on the question of negligence before filing suit. In the event he could not get a medical opinion, he could be charged with filing a frivolous lawsuit.

This could potentially result in Sam paying damages to the defendants. Additionally, his signature on the pleadings that would be filed constituted his legal opinion that the lawsuit was not groundless under the attorney code of professional responsibility. He operated under the assumption that the potential defendants would seek to hold him responsible in the event he could not prove his case.

He finally reached Dr. William Ferguson, an internal medicine specialist who practiced alone in Knoxville. Dr. Ferguson verified that he had some experience in working with deaf students and was generally familiar with the causes of deafness, including the possibility of adverse side effects to Strebucin.

Dr. Ferguson agreed to review the records. Due to the time constraints, Sam decided to drive the records to Knoxville and leave them with Dr. Ferguson.

Sam bundled up the stack of records, asked Alma to call Anne to cancel their appointment, and to call Lynn to let her know that he would be getting home late that night. He headed off toward Knoxville in his old Jeep to pursue the only medical lead he had.

*   *   *

Anne was having serious second thoughts about Sam's ability. He seemed to be particularly adept at pointing out potential problems but not nearly so adept at solving them. She continued to suspect that one of the larger firms would have more access and influence with potential expert witnesses.

Ron was skeptical about the entire undertaking. He also had doubts about Sam's ability. However, he was not even sure that he wanted to pursue litigation if they could afford the best attorney in the country. Consequently, the anxiety and uncertainty were taking something of a toll on Anne and Ron's relationship. Anne resented Ron's lack of interest in pursuing the lawsuit and his concern over the cost. Ron felt that

Anne was being pushy and had no concept of how much money was needed. These concerns manifested themselves in their failure to talk.

Later that day, she called Maurice Washington at West Side Hospital and got the name of his friend, Andy Grayson, in Chattanooga. She called Mr. Grayson and found him to be a fairly young sounding attorney who practiced in a two-man firm in Chattanooga. She explained the situation to him and found him eager to discuss the case with her and made an appointment for the next day. She debated telling Ron about the appointment. She finally decided that she owed it to him.

The hope that Mr. Grayson might prove a better alternative buoyed her spirits somewhat. She got little sleep that night, thinking about all she would tell him.

*   *   *

Sam dropped the records at Dr. Ferguson's office. Dr. Ferguson was not in, but the nurse promised to give him the records at the first opportunity.

Sam left Dr. Ferguson's office at about 5:00 p.m. and started back to Chattanooga. He tried to get the Atkins case off his mind, but he couldn't. He spent the entire two hour drive mentally dictating the proposed complaint. He had numerous decisions to make before filing the complaint. Dr. Kilday and his group would surely be defendants. Other possible defendants were West Side Hospital, Dr. Truelove and Dr. Wilcox.

The thought of suing Dr. Truelove was not attractive. Sam doubted that he had any responsibility for the outcome of the case, but he was afraid to leave him out of the case in the event Dr. Kilday attempted to point the finger of responsibility at Dr. Truelove. In situations like this, Sam had found that it was better to have both defendants in the case and allow them to battle over responsibility. If Dr. Truelove was not present in this case, Dr. Kilday would be free to lay the entire responsibility on him. Sam decided that responsibility had to rule out over emotion. He would include Dr. Truelove, if necessary.

* * *

Andy Grayson's office was on the fifteenth floor of the Lighthouse Insurance Tower in downtown Chattanooga. Anne walked through burled walnut double doors and was greeted by a middle-aged lady with an English accent. "Nice touch," thought Anne.

She took a seat on a leather sofa and picked up a copy of a magazine. She had just turned the page when Andy walked out. Six-feet, four inches tall, dark hair, thirtyish. Dressed about like Anne expected.

Together, they walked back to Andy's office and the sales pitch began. Anne was impressed.

* * *

Alma was getting ready to leave the office for lunch when the phone rang. "Sam Trestle's Office."

"Hi, it's me. Karen."

"Hi Karen, how're you doing? I haven't talked to you in a while."

"I'm fine. I still miss our talks—and seeing you, too."

"Me too. We need to get together more often. I'll never know why you and Eddie couldn't work things out, but that doesn't mean we can't talk."

"Sometimes I don't know either, but maybe it's for the best. Anyway—listen, I know Sam's seeing the Atkins, and I figured you'd want to know, but Anne's going over to see some guy—some lawyer in Chattanooga. I just thought Sam ought to know. Tell Sam that Anne is probably gonna go with the lawyer that seems to want to go after the doctor the most."

"Ummm. Not good. Who is it, do you know?"

"Grayson or something like that."

"Doesn't sound familiar. Maybe Sam will know him."

"I'd better go. I just don't think that'd be the best thing for Anne—I really don't."

"Thanks, honey and you give me a call, or come by and see me, you hear?"

"Okay."

CHAPTER 28

▼

"So—what did you find out from Mr. Grayson?" queried Ron, when Anne returned from Chattanooga.

"I don't know. I think I'm more confused now than I was before."

"What did he have to say?"

"Pretty much the same stuff that Sam did. His office is a lot nicer."

"What did he look like?"

"Actually, he looked pretty nice."

"I had in mind, was he young or old—that kind of stuff."

"Younger than Sam. Like he had a whole lot more money than Sam."

"What about his fees?"

"I was wondering when you'd get around to that. It would be the same—except he wants a whole lot more up front for expenses."

"Did you tell him about Sam?"

"No, and he didn't ask. I just kinda felt like he knew."

"Probably. What do you think of Sam?"

"I don't know—of course, I like him, but I just don't know if he's going to be able to pull this off."

"Me either—But I feel better about him than I do about what I've heard about this other guy. Look, we've got to file suit in eight days—is that what the other guy said?"

"Yeah, but he said it wouldn't take long—he could draw up the papers in a day and file them. Makes you wonder what's taking Sam so long."

"Why don't we see what Sam has to say, and if we're not feeling good, then we'll still have a few days to get your buddy in Chattanooga to file it for us."

"Okay—why don't you call Sam and set up an appointment?"

That afternoon, Sam explained the situation regarding Dr. Ferguson. He hoped to hear from Dr. Ferguson within the next few days, and he would begin drafting a complaint since it would need to be filed in approximately one week. He assured Anne and Ron that he could have the complaint prepared and filed in one day.

On that same morning, Sam finally chased down Dr. Ferguson. He had the same question over the missing records that Dr. Brice had discussed with Sam. In addition, Sam was able to wrench from him the conclusion that Strebucin probably caused the deafness.

A flood of relief settled over Sam's body. This was all the information he needed to justify filing suit. Dr. Ferguson did not absolutely state that he would not testify at trial. With the lack of success in lining up expert witnesses, Sam took this as a yes. He was not sure that Ferguson would be a competent witness since his specialty was internal medicine and Dr. Kilday's specialty was orthopedics, but he had enough information to proceed with filing suit.

He picked up the phone and called Anne. "Anne—good news. Dr. Ferguson has given me enough to go ahead and file suit. I'll begin drafting the complaint today and hopefully we can have it filed tomorrow. Based on my discussions with Dr. Ferguson, Dr. Brice, and my own thinking, I feel like we will need to name Dr. Truelove in the suit. Since he lives here in Marion County, this would give us a basis to file suit in Marion County, and I believe that would be a plus."

"I was going to suggest that you and Ron come by this afternoon to look at a draft of the complaint. I want to make sure that the things we say are factual and we can discuss everything else at that time."

CHAPTER 29

▼

Exhausted, physically and mentally from the lawsuit, school, work and everything else going on in her life, Anne decided to call Karen. She had been Anne's one anchor to a saner world.

"I sure hope things are going better for you than for me," Anne confided.

"I'm sorry—you having a bad day?"

"Bad life would be more like it."

"I'm sorry—can I do anything?"

"I don't know—do you take out contracts on doctors?"

"Sorry, I can't help there. By the way, what did you decide about the other lawyer?"

"I went up to Chattanooga and talked to the guy—but it's just confusing—I don't know."

"What're you going to do?"

"I don't know. I guess Ron and I need to talk to Sam. Sometimes, I'd like to just quit."

"Don't do that. I know it's frustrating—but you and I both know you're going to keep on."

"I guess—sometimes I feel like I'm out here by myself—Ron's about as much help as a rock—and I guess I thought God would pull me through all this—but that's obviously not working."

"Why do you say that?"

"Look at me, I'm worn out, stressed out—my marriage has gone to pot—I don't have any idea what to do with Chad. I'm just lost."

"Things could always be worse."

"Right. There's a great thought. They probably will be tomorrow."

"It's just not like you to give up—"

"You know I'm not giving up—but it really is hard to know what to do—is this the right thing—is that the right thing? Why kid myself?"

"You're just upset—I—"

"Darn right, I'm upset. That's the whole point. Some doctor almost kills one of your kids you'd be upset too. There's no forgiving something like that. He did it and it's over and it's always going to be that way. I hate the guy's guts."

"I don't know about all that other stuff, but this hatred for Doctor Kilday isn't good—it'll eat your insides out."

"Not before I eat his insides out—I can tell you that."

"You just think about it, that's all I'm saying. You better watch where you're going."

"I'm sorry. I guess everything just kinda came spilling out."

"Feel better?"

"No."

"Oh, I was going to say for you just to call anytime and I'd be glad to help out if I can."

"I know—you help as much as anyone could. There just isn't anything to make it go away."

"Call if you need to talk again."

"See ya."

CHAPTER 30

"Grayson? Andy Grayson. He's a good lawyer—and working a bunch of these kind of cases."

Alma relayed the whole conversation.

"So, what're we gonna do? I guess I'm ready to file, but I've got to get Ron and Anne's permission. Maybe I oughta go by their house."

"Sounds like a good idea."

"Why don't you try to get Anne on the phone and I'll try to set it up for this evening."

Sam turned his attention to preparing the papers to file. It was really fairly simple, once you had done the background. Alma buzzed with Anne on the line.

"Hi Anne, it's Sam. I'm working on these papers, and I need to talk to you as soon as I can. Will you be home right after work? I thought I'd drive over if that's okay."

"I guess—but I can come by if you want—the house is a wreck."

"No problem, if you don't mind. I need to be out anyway. And I'd like to meet Chad. You know, I haven't gotten to see him."

Anne was slightly taken aback. "Sure—okay. I should be home from work by a quarter 'til five."

"Good. See you then."

Sam worked on the papers and mentally prepared his approach to Anne. He knew they were going to go with Anne's choice.

CHAPTER 31

"Anne, I've been working solid on the case for the last two weeks, much to the displeasure of my other clients, and after talking to Dr. Ferguson I feel that we've got a solid witness and a solid medical foundation to proceed on. I'm confident about the case. You know most people don't understand that the most difficult part of the case is the preparation that occurs outside the courtroom. Most people think that you just show up and call the witnesses and make a compelling argument at the end. However, I've probably put hundreds of hours into this thing just to get to the point of preparing the complaint. Now, I think all of our hard work is ready to pay off."

Sam had concluded that the primary advantage he could have over another attorney was his personal concern for Chad and his family as a member of the local community and a close family friend.

"Anne, I want you to know that I've invested as much time and energy in this thing as I have because of my personal concern for Chad and your family. We haven't been close personal friends and I know lawyers have to be careful not to get too close or emotionally involved, but I can't help but think in terms of how I would feel if this happened to my own son. And not having any children of my own, I almost feel like I'm fighting this thing as if Chad were my own."

Sam thought that was about as far as he could push it. But he suspected the guilt trip was sufficient to help him keep on the case.

"Also, after talking to Dr. Brice and reviewing the records, its obvious to me that this guy Kilday is a crook. What else could have happened except that he took those records?" Sam narrowed his eyes. "I'd like to get my hands on him. At least we'll have the opportunity to stick it to him in this case."

Within a moment, Sam realized that the case was his. He thought he even detected a trace of tears in Anne's eyes. Whether that was the case or not, she did not mention another attorney nor did he.

Anne had learned to rely on her heart and her intuition in making decisions. She felt that the leanings of her heart subconsciously guided her in the right direction. She concluded that in this instance, although Sam was probably saying this to smooth things over, she didn't believe that he knew about Andy Grayson. Her heart told her even though he was probably laying it on thick for her benefit, that deep down inside he did believe the things he told her. The subject of changing attorneys never came up in their conversation or in Anne's thoughts again. She started to feel closer to Sam and see him in a different light.

CHAPTER 32

Sam walked into his office looking haggard. "You've had a couple of calls from someone, who wouldn't leave a message," said Alma. "I can usually figure out who it is, but I didn't recognize the voice."

"Man or woman?"

"Man."

"Shucks."

"Sounded like somebody local. He said he'd call back later."

Sam slumped in his chair, propped his feet up on his desk, closed his eyes, and caught a few minutes rest. He had not had much sleep for several weeks while trying to work on the Atkins' case and keeping up with his other files.

Alma walked back to Sam's office and dropped a stack of papers on his desk. "You gonna be okay? Do we still have the case?"

"I guess I'm gonna be okay, and yes, we still have the case. Sometimes I wonder why I get into these things. I'm trying to find a doctor that will testify, and no luck. The one key document in the whole case is missing."

"Everything will work out."

"Wish I knew how."

"Doesn't it always?"

"Let me see. Seems like I remember losing a case or two somewhere along the line."

"You dummy—of course you're not going to win every case you get involved in—I mean sometimes they're guilty—but I don't remember any time you'd say you didn't do as well as you could have."

"I don't know about this one—and while I'm spending day and night talking to doctors all over the country, we're getting farther and farther behind on other work. It wouldn't be quite so bad if I could get some of my other work out and get some money in. Maybe I should have brought somebody else in to work on the case with me that specializes in medical malpractice—or I just wish I had Horace here—wonder what he'd do."

"I can tell you what Horace would do. He'd start drinking about 7:00 in the morning, and be half drunk by nine."

"Maybe that's not such a bad alternative."

"I don't know, that's probably one reason why he's not around to help out now. I don't know how he did it, but sometimes he'd spend the night down here—asleep in his chair when I left—and I reckon about midnight he'd have a brilliant idea. When I would come in he'd be asleep in his chair, but there would be a stack of work on my desk. I've driven by here many a time in the middle of the night, and there'd be his light burning back in his office. In the early years I'd stop in and see if I could help, but I finally decided he just needed to be alone."

"It always seemed easier when he was in charge."

"You don't think he had any more answers than you, do you?"

"Heck yeah—and they seemed to work, too."

"Heaven forbid he would have ever heard me tell you this, but he generally didn't know any more about what he was doing than you do. I think he just learned to keep on going on—and let things work out. Sometimes you just don't have a choice."

"It seemed to me that Horace knew a whole lot more about what he was doing...."

"Don't kid yourself. You know twice as much law as Horace did. He just covered it up better than you do."

"Let's see—you're telling me that neither one of us ever really knew what we were doing and that's supposed to make me feel better. Am I missing something?"

"Hey, both of you had one advantage."

"Am I supposed to ask what that was?"

"I'll be more than happy to tell you—me."

"So share some of your wisdom with me."

"Okay. You might consider that the doctor is the one that stands to lose most by the record being lost. I'll bet you that any jury is going to conclude that the records showed something that the doctor didn't want them to show."

"Think so, huh?" Sam had a slight grin.

"Sure—wake up. Juries sometimes are a heck of a lot more interested in what they don't see than what they do see. One thing about Horace—he may not have been the world's greatest legal scholar, but he knew people."

"Guess I'd better get back to pretending I know what I'm doing. Maybe I need a little midnight inspiration."

"Could be."

At 4:00 p.m., Sam had the Atkins' file spread all over his desk and had reached the conclusion that he had exhausted every lead once again.

At 4:30 Alma interrupted. "Whoever it was that called earlier is on the line again."

"This is Sam Trestle."

"Hello, Sammy." Sam recognized the voice of Cliff Hixson. "Hi, what's going on?" Sam realized that Cliff had not identified himself.

"If anybody asks, you don't know who's calling and this conversation never happened, but I've got a name for you," whispered Cliff. "Dr. Damon Cuensler, University of Kentucky Med School. I understand he's a hired gun. A real fruitcake."

"Sounds exactly like the kind of guy I'm looking for. I've already forgotten where that name came from. Seems like somebody suggested him to me, but I can't remember who."

Cliff Hixson had just returned from a medical convention in Memphis. While there, one of his colleagues had talked with him about the horrors of a lawsuit he had been involved in. He described Dr. Cuensler, who had testified against him, in vivid detail. From the description, it seemed that Dr. Cuensler must have fangs and horns growing out of his head. Cliff decided he sounded just like the kind of witness Sam had been looking for.

When Sam ended his conversation with Cliff, he hung up the phone and immediately dialed directory assistance for Lexington, Kentucky.

CHAPTER 33

It was late evening, and Sam, Ron and Anne were working on the case. "I'm going to have to go to Kentucky to talk with Dr. Cuensler. Although he's reviewed the records for us, I need to meet him and talk to him face-to-face."

"What do you want to do?" asked Ron.

"I could either fly or drive up there. Obviously it will take me a lot longer if I have to drive," said Sam.

"I'd like to go along," said Anne. "If we're gonna pay this guy $400.00 an hour to review the records, I want to make sure we're getting our money's worth."

"Of course, you're welcome to go. It might even be helpful if he got to meet you and you got to ask any questions that you wanted to ask."

"How much have we spent on this guy anyway?" asked Ron.

"I would say right around $4500.00. Of course, we'll have to pay him for the time when we're there talking to him, and he gets $500.00 an hour for testifying in court. So, this isn't going to be cheap."

"We might as well go completely bankrupt and fly you and Anne both up there. If you feel like it's important to meet with him, then I'd say let's do it. At least it's a whole lot cheaper than flying him down here."

*   *   *

Anne settled back in her seat as the plane began its ascent from the Chattanooga airport. She did not know how Sam had finally located Dr. Cuensler. Dr. Cuensler's name came to Sam after two other physicians in Nashville had agreed to testify and then suddenly changed their minds. Anne knew that the reason for their change of mind had been word through the medical underground. However, there was nothing anyone could do about it.

Sam got a cup of coffee from the stewardess, took a sip and turned to Anne. "So, how's everything going in your life?"

"Terrible. I had no idea of all the stress we were going to get into. Of course you know Dr. Truelove told us to come and pick up our records from his office. I don't know why that hurts so much. I guess I can understand it, but I guess everybody in Jasper loves him so much that it's just hard to take the rejection. And then of course every time I go out anywhere I get looks from people. I don't know whether it's over the lawsuit or what."

"Yeah—I know what you mean. I get the same thing, but I guess I'm used to it. Seems like as time goes on I've tended to make about half of Jasper mad at me. Of course, that's just the way it goes with my job. But I think everybody will get over it."

"I'm not sure. They may with you because they know it's your job, but if it came down to a choice between us or Dr. Truelove, I think everybody would choose Dr. Truelove."

"I know what you mean. I couldn't believe the guy could be so mean. I felt like I needed to call him before we filed suit. He didn't have much to say but finally told me I might as well start packing my bags because if he had anything to do with it this would be the last case I tried in Jasper."

"Gosh, I didn't know that."

"I figured you had enough to worry about with everything else going on without having to worry about whether the Trestles are going to be able to eat next month."

"In a way it seems like we've almost become hermits. We don't go to church much anymore because I'm afraid we'll run into Dr. George. We don't go out to ballgames or things like that because of the looks we get from people. I tell you it's just about to wear me out. On top of everything else, I'm worried about Ron. He seems to be even more withdrawn, and I guess you can't help but wonder if this whole thing could affect his job."

"Just hang in there. I've never known of a situation where everything didn't blow over. It may take a little while, but as they say, 'this too shall pass.'"

As the plane ended its ascent and leveled out, Anne settled back in her seat. She closed her eyes, leaned back in her seat, and enjoyed the moment of respite from the world of stress that had been engulfing her. When she opened her eyes, she was looking directly at Sam. He was in his seat, just looking at her. Her pulse quickened as she held his gaze and then found herself lost deep in his hazel eyes. She closed her eyes again and leaned her head over. For a few minutes, somewhere in the air, she found contentment.

* * *

Sam and Anne took a taxi to the University of Kentucky Medical Center. They found Dr. Cuensler older than expected, with a full head of white hair, a mustache, and white bushy eyebrows. Sam wondered why Dr. Cuensler was willing to help. He had been around long enough to doubt that it was strictly from a desire to help to the Atkins family. He suspected that Dr. Cuensler was a tenured faculty member, had little use for physician relationships, particularly with physicians in Chattanooga, and finally, Sam concluded that he liked the extra money that came with the work.

"You'll be interested to know that I've already received two calls from colleagues here in Lexington advising of dire consequences if I testify," were his opening words to Sam and Anne.

"How could they possibly know that I'm discussing the case with you?" Sam questioned with disbelief.

"I called Dr. Kilday and talked with him about it, I suppose is how," he said. Sam strained with all of his self control to squelch his rise in temper. He still realized he might need Dr. Cuensler, and he didn't want to alienate him. Dr. Cuensler noticed a change of color in Sam's face.

"I'm not inclined to play these little games with anybody, Counselor. I'll be glad to review the files and give you my honest opinion, so long as you keep paying for it. But, you can't tell me who I can and can't talk with, so if that's not acceptable, you can feel free to find you somebody else to testify."

Sam was speechless. Somehow he admired Dr. Cuensler's forthrightness and saw it as a sign of honesty and objectivity; however, maintaining some semblance of secrecy was important to this case.

"Well, I suppose you don't want to fire me yet so you might as well get your money's worth. The bottom line is this: without the monitoring records, I can't tell you with absolute certainty that Strebucin caused the deafness. There's no doubt in my mind that these records were kept. If they weren't this would be the most blatant case of malpractice that I ever heard of. So, I'm sure they kept records. On the other hand, it doesn't make much sense to think that they did the monitoring but never looked at the results. The whole thing doesn't make any sense. But the only explanation I can come up with is that they just forgot to look. As to what happened to the records, my bet is Dr. Kilday has something to do with their disappearance." Sam and Anne gave each other a knowing glance.

"However, I've been around the game long enough to know what you need me to say. It's my opinion to a reasonable degree of medical certainty that deafness was caused by excessive doses of Strebucin. The only other possible cause would be infection spreading to the ears which caused the deafness. I think the odds are extremely small that this would have happened in both ears. Strebucin is therefore the only other possibility."

"The fact that the records which would establish the levels of Strebucin are missing certainly points further to the fact that somebody doesn't want us to know what those levels were. I'll be glad to testify to every bit of that."

Sam had gone from shock to exultation. His stomach was turning internal somersaults. Dr. Cuensler was the best witness he had ever talked to. He appeared to be forthright, yet not overly anxious to exhibit his expertise.

"Doctor, would you provide me with a written opinion to that effect? The defendants have filed a Motion for Summary Judgment, which means that they are asking to have the case dismissed by showing that it is groundless on the basis of affidavits. Of course, they have filed their own affidavits stating that Strebucin was not the cause of deafness. I will need to take your letter, have it typed up in affidavit form, and have you sign it so that I can file it."

"That would be fine with me, counselor. I would have been surprised if they had not moved for summary judgment. It happens in about every case I'm involved in, and signing the affidavits is just part of the routine as far as I'm concerned."

"If you want me to give a deposition, the cost will be $500.00 an hour and the same cost for appearing in court, starting from the time I leave home until the time I get back. This, of course, will be in addition to air travel and other expenses incurred, and I don't eat cheap." Anne's eyes looked straight at him while her mind began working as a calculator.

Sam nodded and told him he would be back in touch. He knew that Anne was seeing dollar figures; however, he felt that Dr. Cuensler would make an excellent witness and they had no alternative other than to use him, whatever the cost. If they were successful in obtaining a substantial verdict, it would be worth it, whatever the investment.

As they were leaving, Sam thought to ask Dr. Cuensler what Dr. Kilday had said. "I was wondering if you were going to get around to asking me that. He said that the records were kept, that the levels were carefully monitored, and that he kept in touch with it several times a day. He was very aware of the dangers of excessive amounts of Strebucin and he doesn't have a clue as to where the records went. Of course, I don't know what else he could say under the circumstances, but I'll swear the guy sounded sincere."

Dr. Cuensler's evaluation of this situation mirrored Sam's. He was sure that Dr. Kilday would testify that adequate records were kept and that they were all within normal limits. However, no one would have had any reason to want the records to disappear other than Jack Kilday. He had heard stories of disappearing or altered medical records but had never encountered this in his own practice.

Sam and Anne had three and a half hours before their return flight to Chattanooga, most of which they spent eating lunch and chatting on the campus of the University of Kentucky. She found herself a little confused, but increasingly enjoying her time with Sam. They could actually talk.

"How did you think it went with Dr. Cuensler?"

"The first thing I heard about him was that he was a real fruitcake. I don't guess I've seen or heard anything that's changed my mind, but I believe that he will make a good witness. He'll either make a great witness or a terrible witness."

* * *

Anne returned from Lexington, tired to the bone, at 10 p.m. She found Ron in his easy chair watching a ball game on the television. She filled him in briefly, but was too tired to go into detail. She dragged herself upstairs, and managed to get Karen on the phone.

"I'm sorry to call so late, but I've got to talk."

"That's okay. How did everything go with the doctor?"

"Oh, the doctor was okay, but I need to talk about Sam."

"Why? Are you thinking about dropping him again?"

"Afraid not. I think I'm getting…maybe a little, uh…"

"What? Sam? You're kidding."

"No—not kidding. With everything going on in my life, Chad, the case, Ron, and everything else, you name it. The first time I felt real good in months was on the plane, with Sam and the whole world behind."

"Listen, I can understand that, but you've got too much at stake here to get involved with Sam."

"I know. But what do you do? I was sitting there with my eyes closed just enjoying getting away from the world in the plane while it was taking off, and I opened my eyes for a second all I could see was Sam's big eyes. I swear I can't help but like him."

"Great. That's all you need. What's that going to do with the case?"

"Gee, I hadn't thought about that. He sure does have some nice eyes though."

CHAPTER 34

▼

"Not bad at all, Sam my man." Johnny French held his hand over his eyes, squinted and watched Sam's ball glide out the fairway and come to a stop a few yards from the right rough.

"Nothin' to it, my good man."

Johnny and Sam were playing Ralph Dyson and Bud Wilson in a Saturday afternoon grudge match. Dyson was a local real estate agent and Wilson a vice-president at the same bank where Johnny worked. Johnny and Sam were up three dollars.

Sam put the cover on his driver and inserted it in his bag. He propped his foot up on the edge of the cart and reached into his golf bag to get another glove.

"What're you doing?" Johnny was hustling over to the cart.

"Is this a trick question? I'm changing gloves."

"Do I have to tell you everything? You don't change anything when you're ahead."

"You're kiddin', right?"

"No, man—I'm not kidding."

"I've got a hole in my glove."

"We're ahead—just don't change stuff when we're ahead."

"Yo! Up there! You guys gonna sit and talk, or are we gonna play golf?" It was an impatient Wilson, in the cart behind them.

"Yeah, yeah—keep your shirt on—we can't change anything up here without Mr. French's permission."

"Great! Is he giving you the 'don't change anything cause we're ahead' speech?"

"Why? Have you heard that one before?"

"Why do you think we've still got the same old ugly sign up on the front of the bank?"

Johnny threw his head back and took his cap off. "You guys are a real riot."

Sam stepped on the gas pedal. The brake clicked off and the old cart coughed to life. Sam and Johnny rolled off down the cart path, chattering like Abbott and Costello.

"So how's the case goin'?"

"What's that—Anne Marie's case?"

"No, the Lindberg kidnapping case."

"Well, I do have more than one, you know."

"Tell me about the other one later."

"It's goin' okay, I guess—'Bout to run me out of the office."

"Whadda ya mean?"

"Too much to do—I've spent the last six weeks trying to find a doctor to testify."

"Not easy to find, huh?"

"Shoot—you wouldn't believe—"

"So did you get somebody?"

"Yeah, some old geezer up at the University of Kentucky—looks like Albert Einstein or somethin'."

"Is he any good?"

"Who knows? He'll either be real good or real bad. I guess he'll do okay, if he doesn't scare the jury half to death."

"That's real comforting."

"Yeah—but I think he'll be okay."

"How's Anne Marie taking it all?"

"She's taking it all—that's one thing for sure—I swear nothing gets by that girl."

"Yeah. She's pretty sharp."

"Sharp?—She's gonna wear us out—like, I gave her this legal pad—brand new legal pad—and told her to just write down things that Chad can't do now—you know so we could use it for testimony. The whole idea is to give her something to keep her occupied. So here she comes back two days later—got the whole thing filled—'Uh, could we sit down and go through these?'—And I'm like—give me a break."

"Welcome to the world of Anne-Marie."

"What drives that woman?"

"I'd say it's how much she despises the doctor—What's his name?"

"Kilday."

"Yeah, that's it—how could I forget? Anyway, she can't stand the guy."

"I guess that's it—but all in all, I guess she's okay."

"She's 'okay'?"

"Sure, I guess. Why?"

"I'm not going to regret bringing you into this case, am I?"

"Don't think so."

Sam stopped the cart while Dyson hit his second shot, a seven iron that dropped ten feet from the cup.

He started to drive off with Wilson yelling in the background. "Hey Johnny—just don't change anything."

Part III

▼

"The truth? Whose truth are you
talking about? Mine? Yours?
Dr. Kilday's? Whoever took the
record's version of the truth?
No, I doubt that the 'truth'
will have very much to do with it."

Sam Trestle

CHAPTER 35

Sam was in serious preparation for the upcoming trial. He was working late most nights now, toiling over upcoming scheduled depositions.

Wes Howell, Dr. Kilday's attorney, was likewise working late nights. He had enlisted the assistance of one of his partners in outlining questions for the depositions. His firm also had a group of associates, younger attorneys who were just beginning practice, whose work consisted of long hours of legal research and other less enjoyable aspects of case preparation.

Wes also had the benefit of the latest legal research aids on computer. His associates had exhausted every possibility in an effort to find something that would give them an edge.

Sam was preparing for the depositions with Ron and Anne. "The depositions will take place in Wes Howell's office, and your depositions will probably last an entire day."

"Why are we going to Wes Howell's office?" asked Anne.

Sam was slightly embarrassed to admit that he had agreed to take the depositions in Wes's office due to the fact that his office was not large enough to accommodate everyone who would be present.

"There'll be a court reporter who will take down everything that is said. Mr. Howell will ask you questions about the case."

"Who'll be there?" asked Ron.

"Both of you will have the opportunity to be present during all of the depositions, and I believe that would be best. It's usually helpful if the person whose deposition is being taken has to look at the other party. There also will be the court reporter, and Dr. Kilday will have the right to be there during all of the depositions, as will all of the other parties, and their attorneys."

"So, there'll be quite a few people present," continued Sam. "However, it'll be different from the courtroom since it will be done in the attorney's office, and there won't be a judge or jury."

"The important thing for you to remember is that this is Wes Howell's opportunity to find out everything he can about the case. His goal will be to get you to talk as much as possible, and to get as much information as he can get from you about the case."

"Another goal of all the attorneys will be to obtain information which can be used against you at the trial. For example, if you say something that might tend to minimize our damages, this can be used at the trial. What they will do at the trial is bring out your deposition and call your attention to what you said at the depositions, in the event you attempt to change your testimony."

Sam, Ron, and Anne stayed at the office late while Sam put them through the paces of a mock deposition, with Sam playing the part of Wes Howell. When they left, he felt that Ron and Anne were as prepared as possible.

*   *   *

"We've got to discuss how we're going to handle the missing medical records in your deposition tomorrow." Wes Howell and Jack Kilday were also talking about depositions.

"All I know is that they were there when I went down and reviewed the records, and they showed exactly what I thought they should have showed. Why is this a big deal? I thought the fact that the record was missing would help us."

"Just focus on how you're going to answer the questions."

"I specifically remember having the tests run. I was thinking about it last night. I had a little run-in with the staff over getting the tests done. We wanted to get the testing started immediately. Since it was late at night, the lab said we would have to wait until the next day. The shift was changing, or something. I remember telling them we needed the tests then—shift change or not."

Wes wanted to believe Kilday; however, he had growing skepticism. Wes did not relish the idea of explaining to the jury that key medical records, which would have decided the case one way or the other, were missing. Although Wes knew that Anne Atkins had reviewed the records, it seemed extremely unlikely that she could have known and removed the one page that now loomed as critical. And, there was supposed to be a hospital employee with her while she was going through them. And finally, Kilday himself said that the record was still there when he reviewed the records. What else could have happened?

He had other questions as well. Wes was convinced that the child was totally deaf, notwithstanding his client's protestations to the contrary. He suspected that the jury was also going to believe that the child was deaf. From his information, there was no question but that Strebucin could cause deafness. Indeed, Dr. Kilday would have to testify to that.

Dr. Kilday, like Anne, had considered firing his attorney and hiring a new one. However, his liability insurance company would not pay for another attorney. He either had to proceed with Wes and his firm, or pay for his replacement out of his own pocket.

He realized that Wes was a top notch medical malpractice defense attorney, but Wes's apparent lack of belief in him was annoying. Jack Kilday was not used to having to deal with people who did not take his word at face value.

This was one of a myriad of problems Dr. Kilday did not like having to face. He had flown into a rage, both at the hospital and at home, on several occasions since the case was filed. He was moody and had become more withdrawn. The attempts of his wife and partners to console him with the fact that such suits were inevitable, even in the best of situations, had been to no avail. "If we're going to go to trial without you believing my statements, I think you ought to get off of this case and bring somebody in who believes in me. I'm sick and tired of spending all my time working on this case, and I'm particularly tired of having to do it with my own lawyer who questions my story."

Jack Kilday had been one of the biggest problem clients Wes had ever had. He called regularly to discuss annoying details. He dropped by the office unannounced two or three times a week. Dealing with temperamental clients was one of the hazards of Wes's practice. However, he felt that he had probably reached the height of difficulty with Dr. Kilday.

Wes and his partners felt that the case probably should be settled. However, under the terms of Kilday's insurance policy, the case could not be settled without Dr. Kilday's approval, and he was sure that would not be forthcoming.

It was also fairly evident to Wes that his client was the defendant with the most to lose. Although he might try to shift some of the blame to Dr. Truelove, he felt there was little chance of success. West Side Hospital had also been sued, but Wes saw little possibility of shifting the blame in that direction.

Nothing short of a complete vindication would satisfy Dr. Kilday. Wes thought the odds in the case were about even. He had the most articulate client, the most resources and the best expert witnesses. But Sam had, or didn't have, the missing record.

CHAPTER 36

"Doctor, would you agree that monitoring of a patient for levels of Strebucin is extremely important for a patient who is receiving IV dosages of that medication?"

"Yes, I would say that is important," answered Dr. Kilday.

Sam Trestle had been grilling him for three hours in the pre-trial deposition. The previous day, Wes had put Anne and Ron through the same ordeal. Dr. Kilday's annoyance at the whole process was evident. Now, nerves tightened as everyone realized the questioning was turning to Strebucin.

"Was that done in this case?"

"Yes." Dr. Kilday had been forewarned at length to provide only simple, straight forward answers to the questions which were being asked. For this reason, he volunteered no information and answered only in the affirmative.

"Are you aware that there are no records of any such monitoring in the West Side Hospital medical files?"

"Yes, I am aware of that." Dr. Kilday felt the muscles in his body tightening. His leg muscles were already sore.

"Do you have any explanation as to why those records are not there?"

"No."

"Is it not true that you personally reviewed these records in private by yourself after I had requested a copy of them?"

"Yes, I did review them at the hospital. This is not unusual when a request is made by an attorney."

"Did anyone else from the hospital review them to your knowledge?"

Dr. Kilday paused, and tightened again. He looked at Wes Howell and remembered that Wes had also reviewed the records. Wes looked somewhat uncomfortable also. "Tough luck buddy," thought Kilday, "if there was something wrong with your reviewing the records, then I guess that's something you should have thought about before."

"After I reviewed them, Wes Howell reviewed the records."

"And that is your attorney who is with you here today?"

"Yes."

"Do you have any recollection as to what was in the records?"

"They were fairly routine records of monitoring of fluid intake and output. The reason that I wanted to review the records was to just make sure that my recollection was correct, which was that they were always within normal limits. Since I reviewed the records for that purpose, I am very sure that is what they showed."

"So it's your sworn testimony here today that the records were there when you reviewed them?"

"Yes."

"Doctor, do you recall the actual figures that were entered on the records?"

"No, I don't recall the specific numbers, although I specifically recall that everything was within normal limits. This is certainly something I would remember."

"Just so I'm certain that the record is clear, it's your testimony that these records were contained within Chad Atkins medical records when you reviewed them and Mr. Howell reviewed them prior to them being sent to me?"

"Yes."

"And as far as you know, you were the last two people to review the records prior to them being copied and transmitted?"

"I really don't have any way of knowing who had access to the records after Mr. Howell and myself. I also don't know whether someone had access to them between the time that Mr. Howell and I saw them. All I can testify to here today under oath is that those records were in the file at the time I saw the file."

"Do you know whether the records were in the file when Mr. Howell saw them?"

"Obviously I wasn't present when Mr. Howell saw the records so I can't personally tell you about that."

"Have you discussed it with Mr. Howell and has he advised you one way or the other?"

"Mr. Howell has told me that he doesn't know whether they were there at that time or not. His review was just a general review of the record that took only a few minutes and he did not know specifically to look for that particular portion of the records; therefore, he doesn't remember one way or the other."

After a few more minutes of questioning the deposition ended. Sam, Anne, and Ron left to return to Jasper. Wes and Jack Kilday retreated to Wes' office. Kilday had contained himself but was seething inside.

"Why did you just sit there?" You just let him ask those questions that obviously are intended to imply that either you or I removed those records and you didn't do anything. I'm reporting this to the insurance company. At least I would think that anybody could keep some redneck lawyer from making their client look like a complete thief." Wes watched Kilday and his blood began to boil.

However, he collected his thoughts and temper and explained to Dr. Kilday that the deposition was different from testimony in court, and that he had very little control over the questions that Sam asked.

In fact, he had to acknowledge Sam's skillfulness in phrasing the questions. Wes made a note to work at length with Dr. Kilday on how to respond to those questions at the trial.

"We'll spend a considerable amount of time going over your testimony at trial. You need to keep in mind that this was only a discovery deposition and that it will not be presented to the jury unless you testify to something contrary at the trial."

Wes had wracked his brain trying to come up with a way to explain the missing record. His only hope at this time was that the jury would believe Dr. Kilday's testimony. This seemed unlikely, since he didn't believe it himself.

Wes reflected that he might be able to mention the fact that Mrs. Atkins had also reviewed the records at the hospital and that she might have removed that record. However, Kilday's insistence that the records were in the file at the time he reviewed them made that impossible.

Sue Daly had been the laboratory technician present at the most critical time period. As fortune would have it, she had, due to another technician's illness, worked a double shift on the night in which the fluid levels would have been most critical. She had also worked her normal shift the following day. Sue would make an excellent witness. She was approximately forty, professional, attractive, and articulate.

Wes was relatively sure the jury would be skeptical of Dr. Kilday's testimony; however, they would probably be more inclined to believe the testimony of a competent and pretty technician who would appear to have no reason to lie.

Unknown to Wes, Sue Daly was not an entirely friendly witness. She also remembered the night that she had to stay late to run Chad's tests for Dr. Kilday. The laboratory had been short of staff. Two technicians had called in sick. Sue had stayed. However, she had filed the doctor's name in her mind for future reference.

CHAPTER 37

▼

Chattanooga and Jasper are connected by a twenty mile expanse of Interstate 24. They are connected in other ways, of course, in the way that the small towns, like spokes around a hub, are dependent upon and connected with a larger metropolitan area. Residents of Jasper wanting shopping opportunities, jobs, medical care and other necessities and desires of everyday life are often forced to seek them in Chattanooga.

To get from Jasper to Chattanooga along Interstate 24, it is necessary to dip below the Tennessee state line into Georgia. This brief journey into another state is in a sense symbolic of passage into another world.

Jasper is a typical small, southern, country town. The mayor described it rather well. "Jasper is blessed with twelve churches, three schools, three banks, and one traffic light."

The present courthouse, built in 1922, is in the heart of downtown. The rest of the town grew up around the courthouse. There are the usual hardware store, feed store, clothing store, a couple of banks and a cafe or two. There are also the ever-present lawyers' offices, most within walking distance of the courthouse.

The most prominent structures in Jasper are, more or less in order, the courthouse, the Baptist Church, the Methodist Church, the Presbyterian Church and the local schools. Everything else is peripheral to these established icons of the community.

Businesses have come and gone through the years. Originally, they had represented the needs of an agrarian community. As society transitioned, so did Marion County. Now, Jasper has its share of video stores, convenience markets, fast food restaurants, and the inevitable super-discount store. Such commercial ventures have come and gone; however, it is a belief in Jasper that the established icons of this community will remain.

Chattanooga, on the other end of the Interstate 24 continuum, is different. At first glance it might appear to be just a larger, richer cousin to Jasper. Although the relationship and the ancestry are hardly deniable, to conclude that one is merely a larger version of the other is to conclude that America is just a larger version of England. One has become what the other never aspired to be. The two communities, joined by a highway like two balls attached to a string are, in reality, worlds apart.

Chattanooga has its courthouse, its churches, and its schools, but the dominating physical presences in Chattanooga are the tall buildings which house business. Banks, insurance companies, and other monuments to modern day business dominate the Chattanooga landscape.

Chattanooga is old money. It is insurance money, Coca-Cola money, banking money, manufacturing money, and other kinds of business money, but it is old money. Chattanooga is an island of southern gentility, different from much of the rest of Tennessee. Chattanooga could have been lifted up, and transported from Georgia, or perhaps Mississippi. Chattanooga is the deep south, in a way that most of Tennessee is not.

On the eve of the trial, two lawyers, each representative of the city in which he lived, sat in their offices and prepared to do battle in the courtroom. Wes Howell sat in his finely appointed office on the 24th floor of a banking tower, conversing with his client. Both lawyer and client had driven to the office in expensive foreign vehicles. Both wore tailored suits.

Sam Trestle's office was in a small, run down building within rock throwing distance of the Marion County Courthouse. He sat there conversing with Ron and Anne Atkins. All three wore casual shirts and jeans.

It would be hard to say which camp exuded the greatest level of anticipation. The trial was important in both camps. In Jack Kilday's mind, his reputation was on the line. If he lost, the amount of the verdict would be covered by insurance. The monetary outcome of the case was therefore secondary.

For the Atkins, the monetary outcome of the case was also secondary, perhaps more so to Anne than to Ron. While Ron had more successfully submerged his pain, grief, and anger, Anne had sharpened those emotions into a well-honed weapon of revenge. She had progressed beyond allowing herself to be affected by the pain on a daily basis. She had channeled the pain into her desire to destroy Kilday.

Thus were born the well-designed plans for his murder of which she sometimes dreamed at night. Helping Sam prepare for the case and preparing for her testimony became not a difficult task but a consuming passion.

Each of the participants left the respective places of preparation and returned home at approximately 10:00 p.m. Each of these participants in the drama that was to unfold the next day in the Marion County Courthouse was charged with a nervous intensity that could be likened to an electrical charge. If nervous intensity manifested itself like an electrical charge, there would have been visible electrical arcs snapping in the air midway between Chattanooga and Jasper.

The lawyers also felt the pressures of financial success or failure. Trial lawyers are by nature competitive. None of the lawyers wanted to lose the case, just because they didn't want to lose.

Although Jack Kilday was a competitor, this was more than a competition for him. His life's work, his judgment, his training, and his experience were to be judged for all the world to see. The sum and substance of who Jack Kilday was would be judged the next day in a Marion County courtroom.

Anne-Marie Atkins felt something even deeper. She had lost something in Chad's illness far beyond anything Kilday had to lose. Anne's months of pain, hurt, anger, and depression had been stirred in the boiling cauldron of life for months. She felt responsible for Chad's illness. She felt that his deafness was God's punishment for her failure as a parent and as a human being. The jury's judgment would likewise be a judgment of her life, her family, her child, her existence.

Anne got ready for bed and read for a while. Surprisingly, she became sleepy, turned off the light, and drifted off to sleep.

She slept for about an hour. When she awoke, she was a bundle of nerves. She lay in the bed, tossing and turning for another hour and finally gave up. She walked downstairs and found Ron about ready to try to get some sleep.

They talked for a minute and then traded locations in an effort to make it through the long night, Ron heading off toward the bedroom, and Anne settling down on the couch downstairs.

Anne mentally reviewed the last two years, beginning with Chad's illness, the long hours in the hospital, and finally everything that had happened with the lawsuit. She was not sure what had sustained her through it all. She did not know what would sustain them through the coming years.

She finally drifted off to sleep on the couch. She awoke with a start, her heart pumping and her body flooded with tension. As she had for so many other days in the past two years, she pulled herself up off the couch, and plunged into the day ahead.

CHAPTER 38

It was Friday morning, the day of the trial. Sam looked at his watch. Six-fifteen. He was sitting in his favorite chair, finishing off his second bowl of Cheerios, his every day breakfast. The local news was on, but Sam was not really listening.

He heard Lynn bustling around in the kitchen, pouring some coffee. "You planning on drinking this stuff or re-paving the driveway?"

"A little strong for you?"

"I'd say. Hey, do you want one of those energy bars to take with you?"

"I suppose. The Cheerios will wear off about ten o'clock. Bring me a couple, would you?"

"Heaven forbid that they ever quit making Cheerios. Poor thing, you'd starve to death. How you feelin'?"

"Okay, I guess."

"Liar—you look like you're about to die of nerves."

"Alright. Other than that, I'm okay."

"Are you really nervous?"

"Yeah, I'm afraid so."

"Why? You've had a bunch of trials before this one."

"Never had one this big. Never completely tried a medical malpractice by myself before. Going against big-name lawyers from big-name firms in Chattanooga. Anything else?"

"You'll do okay. You always do."

"Man, I hope so. There's a lot riding on it—but you never know."

"What'll happen if you lose?"

"Don't even think about it. I guess Anne would be ready to go after me."

"You won't. When are you leaving?"

"Got to meet Anne and Ron at seven at the office."

"Are they holding up okay?"

"Ron seems to keep going without a lot of ups and downs, and Anne's a one woman dynamo. I guess they're doing as well as you could expect."

Sam slipped on his coat, picked up his briefcase and started for the door. Lynn followed and gave him a kiss.

He stepped out onto the front steps. Not much stirring at this time of the morning. There was a chill in the air. Sam took a deep breath and took in the cool dampness of mid-November. He decided to walk to the office.

His heart was beating faster now as he turned the corner and headed for the office. His case of nerves made him think of his baseball days. He'd get just as nervous back then, stepping into the batter's box, everybody's eyes on him. Nothing to do but walk up and give it your best shot. No questions. No excuses. Just you and the pitcher. Now it was Sam and Wes Howell. No more preparation, no more thinking, no more conferences. Time to hit the ball or strike out.

CHAPTER 39

▼

As she arrived at Sam's office, Anne was in single-minded focus. She had gone over her testimony with Sam eight to ten times in the last two weeks. They had even gone down to the courthouse and rehearsed with Anne sitting in the witness chair.

Sam would mix in a few new questions, to keep her testimony from sounding completely rehearsed. However, he had little doubt about Anne's ability to rise to the occasion.

Sam's mind was running in a million directions, worrying over final details. Dr. Cuensler was in town, ready to testify. Ron had picked him up at the Chattanooga airport the day before. Elaine McWherter from the school for the deaf would testify to the effects of deafness to support the claim for damages. Sam realized that his earlier thoughts about the seriousness of Chad's disability, and thus the amount of damages, had been grossly understated.

Anne and Ron would both testify along with Karen Holland, from her perspective as school guidance counselor. All would testify to the extent of the impact of deafness on Chad's life.

Sam had chosen not to have Chad testify. He felt that the impact of testifying would be too great. He was also concerned that Chad would minimize the extent of his deafness, which could hurt their claim for damages, if the jury felt that Sam was trying to stretch the truth.

Sam, Anne, and Ron managed to spend only a few minutes discussing testimony. The rest of Sam's time was spent rechecking his files and notes to make sure that he had everything and that it was exactly where he wanted it.

At 8:30 they left Sam's office to walk to the courthouse. The sun was warming things up a bit as they walked toward the courthouse.

Sam tried hard to appear calm and collected. He was oblivious to things going on around him. His mouth was dry, and he was full of nervous energy.

Sam walked into the courtroom and then to the counsel table and began to set his files in place. After he had organized his files, he excused himself, made a last trip to the bathroom, to the water fountain, and put a cough drop in his mouth. When he went to Court, he always carried a handful of cough drops in his coat pocket. He had the energy bars in his other coat pocket and he thought he must look like a pack rat.

The courtroom was large, with plenty of room for spectators. It was dimly lit. There was a musty smell, like the smell of old books.

Sam paced the courtroom and chatted with the women in the clerk's office and the deputy sheriff assigned to the court. Anne paced outside in the hall. Prospective jurors began filing in. Ron simply sat in his chair with his hands in his lap.

At five minutes till 9:00 the defendants and their attorneys appeared. Along with them came a staff of paralegals, law clerks, and several others that Sam could not identify. He realized that he was going against all of the resources which West Side Hospital, Dr. Kilday, the insurance companies, and the largest law firms in Chattanooga could muster. He could not help but feel some fear from the array of resources being thrown against him.

The seats in the courtroom had filled with citizens from Marion County who had been summoned for jury duty. Sam had obtained a list of the jury a week before trial. The list gave the address of each juror and his or her employer. He and Anne had gone down the list, noting those that they particularly wanted and those that they did not want. Sam had talked to other local lawyers, trying to get information on the jurors. Alma had exhausted her sources. Sam had even driven by some of the jurors' homes, just to get a better feel. Sam liked to spend as much time as possible in *voir dire*, the process of questioning the jury. Knowing the Judge, however, he knew that his questioning would be limited.

Sam had tried numerous cases before Judge Richard Higgins. Higgins detested anything that tended to drag the trial out. Accordingly, he allowed the attorneys very little latitude in questioning the jury.

Sam and Judge Higgins had never particularly liked each other. This stemmed from Sam's association with Horace Stoneham, who had detested the man when both were in private practice. Although he knew Judge Higgins would not give him any breaks, he also doubted that he would actively seek to keep Ron and Anne from receiving a fair trial.

At 9:05 a.m. Judge Higgins appeared from a door behind the Judges' bench. "Oyez, Oyez, the Honorable Circuit Court for Marion County is now in session, the Honorable Richard J. Higgins presiding, be seated please," the deputy announced. The attorneys stood while Judge Higgins ascended the two steps to the platform where his chair was located. Judge Higgins sat, adjusted his glasses to the end of his nose, and silently studied the court file. Higgins was a large man with a full head of gray hair, which he combed straight back. On the elevated bench, in his black robe, he looked even more imposing. The attorneys and clients remained standing until Judge Higgins took his seat.

"Clerk, call the first case on the docket please," said Judge Higgins.

"James Chad Atkins, by next friends, Ronald E. Atkins and Anne-Marie Atkins and Ronald E. Atkins and Anne-Marie Atkins, Individually v. Jack L. Kilday, M.D., et al, Case No. 1691."

Judge Higgins was all business today. "Probably has something to do with the Chattanooga law firms," thought Sam.

"Is the plaintiff ready?" queried Judge Higgins.

"Yes, Your Honor," responded Sam. Sam thought that his voice had sounded weak. He pulled out another cough drop so that he would be better prepared when called upon again.

Judge Higgins turned to the defense table and asked if the defendants were ready. "Ready, Your Honor," they responded in chorus.

"Okay, Gentlemen. We are going to call twelve jurors and ask them to be seated in the jury box. You may question the jury, but I expect the trial to be moved along. You've already received quite a bit of information on the jury, and I will ask a few preliminary questions, so I want you to keep in mind the need to move this trial on. I expect it to be finished today."

Inwardly, Sam moaned. He had been prepared for Judge Higgins to limit his questions, but this little speech indicated that he would allow only the barest minimum.

The Judge called the names of twelve potential jurors, who arose from the church-like pews in the courtroom and found seats in the jury box. Sam watched their every movement, hoping to pick up something which would help him make his decision.

As the jury entered the jury box, Sam wrote the name of each in spaces he had lined out on a legal pad prior to the trial. He then compared the names to the list of wanted and unwanted jurors. Only three of the jurors who he had decided would be favorable were in the panel of twelve. Five who were deemed unfavorable were on the panel. The other four were unknown. Thus began the jury selection process. As Sam had expected, the entire process took only about forty minutes.

Judge Higgins had allowed him only the most meager of questions. Sam was unable to challenge any of the jurors for cause, meaning that the jurors were simply so biased or incapable they were unable to serve. Judge Higgins had threatened the jurors to such an extent that none would give even a hint of bias.

Sam was allowed to excuse eight jurors without cause. These could be excused simply because he, Anne, and Ron would prefer others. Sam had asked his clients to allow him freedom in selection of the jury. Anne and Ron were quiet. The decisions were Sam's.

He concluded that since they had already decided that five of the jurors were unacceptable, he would use five of his challenges in the hope that he would get a better mix on the next draw. He excused the five, who were replaced by three other unacceptable jurors and two "neutral" jurors. The defendants excused four, who were replaced with two unwanted jurors. The process continued until both sides were out of challenges.

Sam was not at all pleased with the make-up of the jury. There were three whom he and the Atkins had concluded were bad choices. The selection process had terminated with only two that they had wanted.

The trial began with Sam's opening statement. He had worked on it for days, including times he had rehearsed in his car, or sitting in his chair at home supposedly doing something else.

"Ladies and Gentlemen, my name is Sam Trestle. I'm an attorney practicing here in Jasper. Prior to Mr. Stoneham's death, I practiced with him for several years.

I must tell you that I feel a tremendous burden in presenting this case to you today."

"Objection, your Honor, this is supposed to be an opening statement made for the purpose of showing what counsel intends to prove, not an opportunity to make an emotional appeal to the jury." The interruption came from Wes Howell. As soon as Wes had objected, Sam wished that he had not started as he had. He had hoped that the defendants' attorneys would allow him some latitude. He now regretted his naïve assumption.

"Sustained," bellowed Judge Higgins. "Mr. Trestle I think you've tried enough cases to know that this is not a time to make an emotional argument. Please state the facts of your case as quickly as possible. I'm going to allow you five more minutes."

Sam's stomach was in his throat. There was no way he could make his opening statement in five minutes. He had no choice other than to try to hit the high spots and hope that Higgins would allow him to exceed the stated time. He knew there was no need objecting, as the Judge would just count the time he spent objecting as part of his five minutes.

Anne was demoralized by Sam's apparent lack of competence and the way in which Judge Higgins had rebuked him. She again began to wonder about Sam's capability to try a case of this magnitude against this opposing small army.

"I apologize, Your Honor, for getting carried away. We intend to show today that prior to the day he entered West Side Hospital, Chad Atkins was a very healthy, normal ten-year-old boy living here in Jasper in Marion County. Several days prior to that date, Chad's parents began observing him having some problems in his shoulder. Chad complained of tenderness in his shoulder. His parents observed him having trouble playing Little League baseball, and they finally took him to see Dr. Truelove here in Jasper."

"Dr. Truelove saw him for several days and then referred him to Dr. Jack Kilday. Dr. Kilday is the dark-haired gentleman sitting over at this table."

"Dr. Kilday saw Chad and his mother, Anne, on two occasions. He ordered x-rays to be done of Chad's shoulder. He also prescribed some anti-inflammatory medication."

"We believe the evidence will show that Chad's condition did not get better. We further believe the evidence will show that Mrs. Atkins inquired of Dr. Truelove's office on a number of occasions and was assured that Chad would get better, but he did not. He continued to show signs of illness."

"All of this came to a head on a Sunday morning. Mrs. Atkins finally realized that Chad was getting worse and took him to West Side Hospital in Chattanooga. There he was admitted through the emergency room under the care of Dr. Kilday. He finally arrived in the pediatric care unit, where he was treated for several days without success."

"Dr. Kilday finally chose to do a surgical procedure where he opened the shoulder area, drained it of infectious fluid, and inserted a tube through which an antibiotic medication was administered directly into the shoulder."

"It is our contention that this medication caused the damage to young Chad in this case." Judge Higgins looked over the top rim of his glasses and spoke, "Very well Counselor, I've allowed you to go over your time a little bit, but I think that will be sufficient. Do the defendants wish to make an opening statement?"

"Your Honor if I could just have one or two more minutes, I've really not had time enough to outline my case." Sam tried not to sound as if he was whining.

"Counselor, you've had as much time as the Court generally allows. I'll give you no more or no less than I give the other side to make a statement of their case. I've reviewed the Complaint in this case and I feel that you've said all that needs to be said. Now, which defendant wishes to begin?"

Sam felt as if he had been slugged in the stomach. His opening statement was the barest of outlines, touching only on the first part of the case. He had not been able to comment on Chad's injuries, the extent of his deafness, or any number of other things which could have helped the case. Even more critical, he had not been able to comment on the blood monitoring or the missing records.

Ron and Anne looked puzzled. In the first two things he had said to the judge and jury, Sam had been embarrassed by the Judge. Sam made a mental note that he should not underestimate Judge Higgins' negative feelings toward him, and how they might affect the case.

Anne was confused but not alarmed. Sam was not showing his concern and Anne did not realize that Sam's game plan had been interrupted. She glanced at Ron. She never understood how men could appear to be so unconcerned. She knew that Ron had the same gamut of emotions and worries that she did. He just seemed to hide them better.

Wes Howell rose to make an opening statement on behalf of Dr. Kilday. Sam thought, "Now that Judge Higgins has cut me off, he'll realize that he only has five minutes also. He'll be able to condense his opening statement so as to hit only the high points in quick fashion."

"Members of the jury, my name is Wes Howell and I represent the defendant, Dr. Jack Kilday. It's my job now to tell you the rest of the story. I'd like to begin by telling you several things that will not be in controversy here today. First, we might as well get out of the way the fact that young Chad Atkins did have a serious, life-threatening illness. I wouldn't argue with Mr. Trestle at all on the fact that he was an active, healthy youngster before this illness. As a result of the illness, he now has a hearing impairment. This is unfortunate, and no one, other than Chad's family, feels worse about it that Dr. Kilday, who has given his entire life to try to help people like Chad. So I think we can all agree and get out of the way the fact that we all have a great deal of sympathy and concern for the Atkins family." The jury smiled and nodded in agreement.

"However, our system of law does not allow every family who has a member with an unfortunate illness to sue that doctor. Our system of law understands that everyone who is born on this planet is going to die. Some are going to suffer illnesses, like Chad, which could cause them to die unless they receive medical treatment. Along the way, some of these accidents and illnesses cause damage to our bodies. However, since death, illness, and accidents that result from these things are part of life, we don't sue the doctor every time we get sick."

"Fortunately, in this case, the evidence will show that Dr. Kilday did nothing wrong to this child. He saved his life. The evidence will show that the child was given a medication which did heal his disease, and which, as a potential side effect could cause some hearing impairment.

However, this medication was given appropriately and what actually caused the hearing impairment was the disease itself."

"Unfortunately, the one document which would have very clearly shown that the medication was given properly has disappeared from the file. Sometime after Chad's care, it disappeared. I suppose it could be said that there might be a number of different people who would have a reason for its disappearance; however, I doubt that we will find out here today what happened to the document. Fortunately, we do have a number of people on the hospital staff who can testify that it showed the medication was given properly."

"In conclusion, and I hate to have to come down here and say this, although Dr. Kilday has no choice but to be here since the Atkins have seen fit to sue him, what we have is someone trying to cash in on the unfortunate tragedy of this young man and his family."

Howell looked directly at Sam. "What we really have is an illness and a limited hearing impairment which resulted from that illness. We think it is true that Chad does not hear as well now as he did before. However, the extent of his hearing impairment is being exaggerated greatly. I'll leave it for you to decide why that is." Howell again looked at Sam.

Sam tried to look unaffected by the attempt to cast him as the villain. He knew that the defendants could not risk trying to make the Atkins look like villains. The jury would extend them a great deal of sympathy and it would be natural for them to seek help. Sam, on the other hand, could safely be cast as a villain who would have every reason to exaggerate the facts in order to line his own pockets. Sam felt it was important not to let the jury think that Howell's tactic had bothered him. He shook his head in disbelief and continued making notes.

"There is much, much more that I could tell you about the details of this case, but in order to keep it as brief as possible, I'm going to end and sit down now. Thank you for your attention."

The other opening statements were similar. Short, sweet, to the point, and effective. All the defendants alluded to the missing medical records.

Apparently, the defense attorneys had learned, as Sam had, that weaknesses in the case needed to be addressed early so that it would appear that there was nothing to hide and that the issue was being addressed openly and candidly.

Anne was shaken by the defense statements. Since there were four defendants, each got to speak as long as Sam, and therefore the defense attorneys had gotten four times as long to reiterate their side of the case. Having heard the accusations which they made, Anne began to question her own motives and sincerity. Were they really trying to make a mountain out of a molehill?

Anne had lost the ability to think or reason. On one hand she almost wanted to forget about the case. On the other, she knew that they had come this far, and she wanted to see it through to the end.

The last defense attorney took his seat. "Call your first witness Mr. Trestle," Judge Higgins thundered from the bench. Sam had expected the Judge to call a short recess. They had been in court well over an hour and he typically allowed the jury to get a break, and himself an opportunity to go to the bathroom, before they began the long process of hearing testimony.

Having assumed that a break would be forthcoming, Sam was slightly off guard. "We will call Anne-Marie Atkins as our first witness, your honor." Sam reached down and helped Anne out of her seat. Anne was scarcely aware of seeing objects in the courtroom. Sam started her toward the witness chair.

Ron reached and took her hand. The touch of Ron's hand upon hers became the only sensation of which she was aware. She wanted to just forget the whole thing, sit down with him, and let him hold her. Sam hesitated a moment and guided Anne toward the witness chair. All eyes in the courtroom were directed toward her. She was all alone in the cold isolation of the witness chair.

CHAPTER 40

Sam Trestle had tried a number of jury cases over the years. If he had ever been able to calm a witness, this was the time. Unfortunately, he was frantically trying to find a way to calm himself. He knew he had started poorly. The points Wes had made rang true. Slowly, he walked to his notebook, turned to the section which outlined the questions he intended to ask Anne, and walked to the podium where the lawyers stood when they questioned witnesses.

"At least he looks like he knows what he's doing," thought Anne. She struggled to find some comforting thought to grasp.

"Would you state your name for the record?"

"Anne-Marie Atkins."

"Where do you live, Anne?"

I live on a farm right outside of Jasper."

"Are you nervous today?"

Anne tried to smile. "Yes, I'm pretty nervous."

"Have you ever testified in court before?"

"No."

"Would it help if you had some water to drink?"

Anne's mouth was so dry she thought it was going to stick together. "Yes, please."

Sam poured Anne a glass of water from the pitcher which sat on his table.

"Your Honor, may I approach the witness to give her this glass of water?"

"Surely," responded Judge Higgins. Judge Higgins realized that Sam was dragging this out as much as possible in order to allow Anne's nerves to settle a bit. Sam figured that he had probably delayed as long as he could; however, he moved as slowly as possible in taking Anne the glass of water. Then, his eyes met Anne's, just as they had that day on the plane. "The truth is always in the eyes," he thought. He was going to be okay. They smiled, slightly, as Sam continued.

"How many people are in your family, Anne?"

"There's my husband Ron and myself and we have two children, Chad and Alan."

"I'll not be so rude as to ask your age, but could you tell me the children's ages?"

"Chad is seven and Alan is five."

"And how long have you lived in Marion County?"

"I've lived here all my life."

Anne knew she was rolling now.

Sam suspicioned that he had taxed Judge Higgins' patience past the limit so he decided to begin serious questioning. "Did your son, Chad, experience an illness last year which has formed the basis of this case?"

"Yes."

"Could you tell me when you first noticed something wrong with Chad?"

Sam led Anne through the entire story of Chad's illness, just as she had related it to him on that very first day. Anne's description of the facts of the case took over an hour. Sam had decided to conclude with Anne's description of the extent of Chad's deafness.

"Ms. Atkins, finally, I would like for you to describe to the court and the jury your observations of Chad and how he can communicate since the onset of the problem that you have described."

"When we were first in the hospital, I noticed him looking at me real funny when I talked to him. I remember right at first when we went back into the intensive care unit, and were trying to talk to him and it was—uh—hard to make him understand. Finally, it dawned on me that he couldn't hear me. At first I just thought it was grogginess from the medicine or something. Then, when we went home it seemed to continue. At first I didn't think that it was too bad. He seemed to be able to communicate to some extent and I kept thinking that it was getting better."

"After watching him several times with sounds around him, I realized that he couldn't hear much of anything. I think he gets along at home and—uh—he can fake it to some extent because he knows the routine and can communicate with us through body language and since he pretty well knows what I want just by looking at me."

"Could you describe some of the incidents where you say you concluded that he couldn't hear?"

"One thing that really sticks in my mind was when the boys were shooting fire crackers. Alan had lit a fire cracker very close to Chad, but Chad didn't see it. It went off right at his feet and I noticed that he didn't jump or anything. He just kind of looked in that direction. Since then I've noticed that he never responds when the telephone rings. As time went on, I've tried just calling his name when he's in the room and he doesn't respond."

"Have you had any tests of Chad's hearing performed?"

"Yes, after a while I was worried about it. Of course, some tests had been done at West Side, but I wanted to get an independent test. So, I took him to Knoxville to the Tennessee School for the Deaf."

"Do you know what kinds of tests were performed there?"

"I don't know all of the tests, but I do know that they did an audiological test which measures his hearing."

"And do you remember who did that testing?"

"Yes, it was an audiologist named Will Fox."

"And do you know if Mr. Fox is present today?"

"Yes, he is."

"What effect has this had on Chad in his daily life?"

"It's really devastating. He simply can't communicate with anyone other than his family. He can communicate with us, as I said before, with facial expressions and body language, but that's about it."

"Insofar as his daily life, it has basically isolated him from the world. He used to be a happy, healthy—just a normal kid. He always had friends over to our house or he would go to their houses on weekends and stuff like that during the summer. Since he lost his hearing that hasn't happened at all. Obviously, he can't communicate with his friends and he's cut off from them."

CHAPTER 41

The trial had broken for lunch and Anne, numb with tension and exhaustion, had been able to eat only a few bites. Sam tried to force himself to put something in his stomach to brace himself for the rest of the day's trial.

The morning's session had gone reasonably well after a rocky start. However, he realized that the first witnesses were the easy part. Anne had performed magnificently. Will Fox had testified to the results of his audiological tests. However, the hardest part would be the medical testimony which would take place that afternoon.

As the trial reconvened, Sam called Dr. Damon Cuensler. Dr. Cuensler testified to his opinion as he had expressed it to Sam and Anne that day in Lexington. It was now time for him to be cross-examined by the defense attorneys. The success of their case would probably hinge on Dr. Cuensler's ability to withstand the cross-examination.

"Dr. Cuensler, have you seen Chad Atkins?"

"Yes, I saw him at my office in Lexington on one occasion." Sam breathed a sigh of relief. It had been expensive for Ron and Anne to take Chad to Lexington to be examined by Dr. Cuensler, but that one question had made the trip worthwhile.

"What treatment have you been providing for Chad?"

"I only saw Chad for the purpose of making an examination of his condition. I am not following him for treatment."

"I'm sorry, sir, did you say that you were not treating Chad in any way?"

"That's right."

"Then for what purpose did you see him? I thought that doctors saw patients for the purpose of treating them."

Sam wrestled with standing to object. Obviously Dr. Cuensler was being portrayed as someone interested only in testifying at trial for the money.

"I saw Chad at the request of his parents to do an evaluation of his condition. It was my understanding that they differed with the treatment and diagnosis which Dr. Kilday had made. They were seeking my advice on a proper diagnosis and evaluation of his condition and recommendations for further treatment. Since I practice in Lexington, Kentucky, it's not feasible for me to provide treatment. However, since I have made a specialty in the study of this kind of condition, sometimes people come to me for second opinions and for assistance to their physicians in diagnosis and evaluation."

Sam sighed inwardly and smiled for the jury.

"Is it not true, doctor, that you saw Chad Atkins solely for the purpose of coming here to testify in this lawsuit today?"

"No sir, that's not true. I was aware that there was a lawsuit pending and I was advised that I might be requested to participate. However, I've spent my medical career devoted to patients. As you can probably tell from looking at me, that's been a fairly long time. Over the years, I've learned to make it a practice not to shy away from cases in the event there is a lawsuit pending. I'm also not afraid to give my opinion to anyone that needs it."

"I don't think that the Atkins should be prevented from getting another opinion simply because they have filed a lawsuit and differ from their first physician over the care of their child."

Sam was trying not to appear too pleased, although he allowed himself another long glance at the jury.

"Doctor, you are no doubt aware of the missing records relating to blood monitoring, are you not?"

"Yes sir, I am aware that there are no records in the file."

"So, you have no way of knowing the results of blood monitoring?"

"I have no way of knowing whether blood monitoring was done, and if it was done I have no way of knowing the results."

"So, you cannot tell us with absolute certainty here today that an excessive amount of Strebucin caused Chad Atkins' deafness, can you?"

Sam had anticipated the question. He sprang to his feet. "We object to that question, your Honor. It's not necessary for the doctor to testify to absolute certainty. The standard is whether it is his opinion to a reasonable degree of certainty."

"Overruled, I'm going to allow the question. Go ahead and answer the question, sir."

"In my field, it is usually impossible to draw any conclusions to an absolute certainty. So, I cannot say with absolute certainty that is the situation in this case."

"And would it not be true that if some other doctor knew that those blood monitoring reports were within normal limits, that physician could say with absolute certainty that the physician administering the medication was not negligent in administering the medication?"

Sam again objected and was overruled by Judge Higgins. He had to make the objections, although he was concerned that his objection and the ruling by Judge Higgins simply underscored the importance of the question and the point which the attorney had wished to make.

"I suppose that's true," responded Dr. Cuensler, "although, as I said, I'm not sure that anything is an absolute certainty in this profession."

The other defense attorneys pounded Dr. Cuensler on basically the same points. Finally, mercifully, Dr. Cuensler's testimony was complete. Sam asked him to stay until the end of the trial in the event he needed to re-call him. The result was another several thousand dollars in expense, but Sam was afraid to take the chance.

Sam glanced at Anne. She had been hit hard by the cross-examination of Dr. Cuensler. To this point, she had focused on her own testimony and their case. She had not been prepared to hear the defense articulate its side of the story. It had surprised her to realize that the defense had a strong, well-articulated, and well-reasoned position. It infuriated her that Dr. Kilday had done something with the missing record and was now capitalizing on it in the presentation of the case.

She began to feel doubts about their case. Was it really as simple as Wes Howell said? She reflected on the fact that she was being represented by a local attorney. She had known Sam since high school, and now they were going up against some of the most experienced attorneys in Chattanooga.

Sam's next witness was Elaine McWherter from Tennessee School for the Deaf. Sam hoped that Elaine could educate the jury regarding the effects of deafness and enhance the claim for damages.

"Ms. McWherter," Sam began, "are you familiar with Chad Atkins?"

Ms. McWherter appeared calm. "Yes, I am. I met Chad when he visited our campus several months ago. He and his mother came to have some testing done."

"Have you had an opportunity to review the audiological test reports which Mr. Fox discussed with the Court earlier today?"

"Yes, I have. I reviewed them with Mr. Fox and Ms. Atkins the day the testing was done."

"Based upon that testing, would Chad qualify for admission to Tennessee School for the Deaf?"

"Yes, he would. Chad would be considered to be profoundly deaf, and if he were referred to our school, he would qualify in terms of the level of his hearing."

"Based upon your experience as an educator of the deaf, are there any unique problems which the deaf encounter in gaining an education?"

"Yes, there are. Our entire system of learning is actually sound based. Our alphabet is based upon the sounds of the letters and the sounds of the words they make."

Elaine was just getting warmed up. "Since the deaf can't hear, it makes it considerably more difficult for them to learn to read. Basically our entire system of learning is based upon the ability to read. If you can't read well, you can't learn English as well, not to mention other languages. You can't learn history, or any other subjects as well as those who can hear."

"Are there any other ways in which deafness affects the educational process?"

"Studies have shown, and our experience bears out, that a large part of learning comes through what we call incidental learning. This is knowledge that we just pick up from exposure to other people and other sources, such as radio and television. For example, when relatives come to visit, children pick up a whole world of information, such as how to behave in social situations, from just listening and observing. It's amazing how much children pick up from radio and television, although some of it, I suppose, we would just as soon they didn't pick up."

"What is the likelihood of a deaf student being able to graduate from college?"

"Nationwide, only a small percent of deaf students complete college. The tremendous disadvantage which they face makes it almost impossible for them to catch up."

"What kinds of jobs are your students able to obtain when they get out of your school?"

"The job market is severely limited for deaf students. Since so many jobs require the ability to hear, the market is severely limited."

The cross-examination was limited. Sam had decided that this was a good place to conclude his case. He had established Chad's problems and that Dr. Kilday was responsible for them. He felt that he had also impressed the extent of Chad's damages upon the jury.

CHAPTER 42

The defense countered immediately with Dr. Kilday. He was obviously well prepared. He appeared soft spoken, humble, and ultimately concerned with the care of his patients.

He testified at great length and detail about his care of Chad Atkins. He appeared near tears in his concern over the absence of the medical record. Once again he swore his innocence in the disappearance of the record.

Wes Howell closed his examination of Dr. Kilday with questions about the cause of Chad's deafness. "Dr. Kilday, in your professional opinion, and to a reasonable degree of medical certainty, can you give us your opinion as to whether Strebucin is the cause of Chad Atkins' deafness."

"As Dr. Cuensler testified, often times in our profession, and this is particularly true of those of us who are actually seeing and treating patients regularly, it's difficult to draw absolute opinions. However, in this case I can tell you with absolute certainty, and with no reservations that Strebucin did not cause this child's deafness."

"Why do you say that, doctor?"

"I was very much aware of the potential side effect which Strebucin can have on a patient's hearing. I would like to take a second to say that the side effect which would normally be expected would not be deafness, but simply some effect on the level of hearing which is what we have seen in this case. However, I was very well aware that this was a possible danger, and for that reason I instituted monitoring at the very earliest point and continued it throughout in order to assure that would not happen in this case. If this is done, it is really a very simple matter to ascertain whether too much of the medication is being absorbed. I checked the test results at least twice a day myself and the nursing staff checked them regularly. I can assure you that those tests were within normal limits at all times."

Dr. Kilday had sounded convincing. He looked sincere. Wes had done his job.

"Now, doctor, I want to ask you a few questions about Chad's actual hearing impairment." The defense team had been careful throughout to refer to Chad's problem as an impairment rather than deafness.

"Have you reviewed records and examined Chad's testing in regard to his hearing? If so, please tell us what you found."

"I have done testing myself and I have reviewed all of the testing which was done, both by our hospital which was providing treatment for Chad, and the other testing as portrayed by the plaintiffs and their witnesses. In my opinion Chad has a considerable amount of hearing. His hearing is not nearly as bad as Mr. Trestle would like to portray."

"How do you explain the apparent differences in the testing?"

"It is not unusual for us to see parents, in their natural concern over their children and in their anger, to exaggerate the extent of these kinds of problems. Obviously when testing is done, and particularly when done at the request of those concerned and angry parents, the test results are often exaggerated."

"I also believe that as Chad continues to recover, that we will continue to see progress in his hearing levels. I think it is likely that he will be hard of hearing for the rest of his life. As an adult, he may need to use a hearing aid as many people do. However, I see no reason why he cannot lead a full, rewarding, and happy life." Howell ended his questioning.

Sam was relieved that he had kept Dr. Cuensler to respond to this line of questioning. But now he had to cross-examine Dr. Kilday. His performance would be critical.

"Dr. Kilday, you specifically remember that the missing medical records were once in the file, is that true?"

"Yes, that's true. I certainly remember seeing them while the child was in the hospital and I also recall seeing them afterward."

"In fact, after I requested the records, you made a special point to go review them, did you not?"

"Yes, that's true."

"And in fact, you made a special point of reviewing them by yourself behind closed doors, did you not?"

"I did not make a special point. I went to the hospital record room because I was concerned about this patient. If there was anything that I had done wrong, or if there is anything that could be done for this child, I wanted to be the first to recognize it. When I went to the records room, I was provided an office and used that office for the purpose of privacy where I reviewed the records."

"Whether you made a special point or not you nonetheless looked at the records by yourself, behind a closed door, is that not correct?"

"Yes, that is correct."

"And it's your testimony here today that the missing records were present in the file at that time, is that not true?"

"Yes, that's true. I specifically remember reviewing those records because I felt that they were particularly important in illustrating the appropriate care which the child received."

"And after that time you cannot account for the whereabouts of the record."

"I have given that considerable thought because if there was any possibility that those records could be found I wanted to find them. I've tried to talk with everybody on the hospital staff and I feel like at this point that there are two possibilities. First, it is not at all unusual for other people in the hospital to review the records. At your request, the record was removed, each page was taken out and copied and the record was disturbed then. The record remained out of its normal spot at the receptionist's desk in the hospital record room for a considerable period of time. I think it is entirely possible that in all of the shuffling of the records that those particular portions of the record were misplaced."

"I think it's also improper that the records were left unattended on the receptionist's desk. I think it's very possible that the record may have been tampered with after I saw it, or that it may have been lost in the process."

"The fact remains, doesn't it doctor, that insofar as you can testify here today, you are the last person who saw that record."

"No, I don't think that's true. I'm quite sure that the young lady in the medical records office saw it, and as I've just said, I think it's entirely possible that you saw it."

"You cannot testify here today that the young lady in the medical records office who made the copies saw it, can you?"

"I obviously can't testify to what she saw or did. I can say without any doubt that the record was in the file when I last saw it. I have no way of knowing who saw it after I did, but I'm sure that it was in the file when I returned it to the desk."

"Also, as I've said, it remained on the desk in the receptionist's office for a considerable amount of time. It's obviously possible that someone entered the office and removed the record after I had access to it."

Sam decided to leave the medical records issue, try to regain his composure, and come back to it later. He led Dr. Kilday through the warning instructions which accompanied the medication, grilled him at length over the extent of Chad's hearing loss, and appeared to make no ground. He was feeling sick at his stomach.

"Dr. Kilday, you don't claim to be a specialist in the area of hearing, do you?"

"My specialty is not in that field; however, my medical training covered the ear and the evaluation of patients with hearing impairments. It also covered the reading and evaluation of audiological testing. For that reason, I am competent by reason of training and experience to make the conclusions and evaluations I have here today."

"Your Honor, could I have a moment to confer with my clients?" Sam was groping for time.

"Make it quick, Mr. Trestle. We've got a lot of ground to cover here and I'm determined to finish this trial today. I have a full docket."

Sam would have liked a recess to collect his thoughts but was afraid to ask for it. He also felt that it would underscore his confusion and frustration in trying to cross-examine Dr. Kilday. He leaned over to talk to Anne and Ron. He really had nothing to say to them since he knew that it was up to him to come up with the questions.

"Do you think there's anything we've left unasked?" Sam mumbled. He was trying to regain his composure. Thoughts raced through his mind, but nothing of significance surfaced.

Ron had the only expressible idea. "He's the only person who stands to lose from the loss of that record. I don't think he ought to be able to just sit there and say it's too bad it got lost."

Sam had no better idea. He returned to the podium. "Doctor, with everything that's been said here today, the fact remains that you're the one person who stands to gain the most by the disappearance of the record, aren't you?"

Dr. Kilday paused. Sam could detect the rising anger in his countenance. Wes Howell stood and objected.

Dr. Kilday's testimony had far exceeded Wes Howell's expectation. Kilday could sense that his testimony had been well received. Dr. Kilday had felt a mounting sense of confidence as he had proven, line by line, that Sam Trestle was the incompetent, money grabbing country bumpkin that he believed him to be. He saw the chance to close for the kill.

"No, Mr. Attorney, I don't think I am the one who stood to benefit from the disappearance of that record. I believe you're the one who stood to benefit. I also think Mr. and Mrs. Atkins and their family stood to benefit."

Wes Howell objected again to halt Dr. Kilday's monologue. He had no problem with the statements that he had made, perhaps in anger and in the tenseness of the situation, but he felt uneasy that Dr. Kilday was taking it upon himself to go beyond the testimony which they had carefully rehearsed.

"That's okay, Mr. Howell, I don't mind answering his question at all. The medical record was sitting on the desk unattended for a long period of time. That receptionist, I observed, doesn't stay where she should all the time. I saw her drinking coffee and chatting with other employees when she should have been tending to business. It's entirely possible that you or someone you sent removed that record."

"I know you've talked to just about every doctor in the Southeast trying to find somebody to testify against me before you finally found the old guy at the University of Kentucky, who probably hasn't seen a patient in years. I probably make more in a month than the professor makes in a year, although I'm sure he's made a bundle off of you."

Wes Howell was punctuating every sentence with objections, but to no avail. Kilday was on the verge of hurting himself.

Sam needed to keep Dr. Kilday going. He glanced at Judge Higgins who appeared to be amused and interested.

"So, is that what this is about? Should we just find out who makes the most money?"

Wes Howell jumped up again objecting. Judge Higgins sat forward in his chair and opened his mouth, but he and everyone else in the courtroom were interrupted by Dr. Kilday.

"That's okay, Mr. Howell, you've done enough. I don't mind answering. I'm sure that I make more money than you've ever thought about making Mr. Trestle."

"I'm sure that whatever doctors you talked to told you that record was important. So I can't see any reason why it would disappear other than that you or Mrs. Atkins had something to do with it."

"It was obvious she never liked me. She probably saw right from the start that this would be a good chance for her to get rich. I suppose in their minds both of them can just retire and live off what they can get off of me."

"And I don't intend to be brought out here in the middle of nowhere to answer about some missing records." Kilday got up from the witness chair, walked over to the table, picked up his briefcase, and walked to the door. He opened the door and walked through. No one moved. The door opened again and Kilday re-entered.

"Mr. Howell, I'll let you and the other bunch of flunkies take it from here. I'm through." The door closed and Kilday disappeared.

Sam was still standing. He had a wry grin on his face. "Uh—no more questions, your Honor." He started back to his chair.

Wes Howell rose from the defense table. "Your Honor, could we have a brief recess?"

Sam thought he detected a slight amused smile on Judge Higgins' face. "Very well," he muttered.

Sam hurried from the courtroom. He wanted to see if Dr. Kilday had left the courthouse. He saw no trace of him.

During the break, the defense attorneys huddled in a remote corner, in obvious panic. Sam wondered what they would do to salvage the situation. They couldn't ask for a mistrial since it was their own witness who had caused the outburst.

Sam, Ron and Anne were together at the table in the courtroom. "I think that his outburst will generally help us, but I am somewhat concerned about Kilday's testimony that Chad really hasn't had that much of a hearing loss."

Anne looked shocked. "You're not telling me that the jury is going to believe him?"

"Well, I would certainly hope that they wouldn't, but he has testified to that and legally there is evidence in the record that they could believe if they choose to."

"Well, what do you think we ought to do?" asked Ron.

"We have the opportunity to put on some rebuttal evidence after they've put on their case. This means we could offer witnesses to contradict things that they've testified to in their case."

"Who do you think we could use to contradict his testimony? We've already used the people from TSD and Dr. Cuensler."

"I don't know. We'll just have to think about it and decide when we get to that point. I could use one of our lay witnesses like Anne or yourself to talk about your observations about Chad's hearing. But let's just wait and see what they do and then make up our mind at that time."

In a few minutes Judge Higgins emerged from his office, and without looking at any of the attorneys, made his way back to the bench.

"We would like to call Gloria Sharp," Wes informed Judge Higgins. Gloria Sharp was the receptionist in the medical records office at West Side Hospital. She testified that she simply copied all of the material in the file and sent it to Sam. She was unaware that any records were missing. On questioning by Mr. Howell, she had to admit that mistakes were made and it was possible that some of the records may have been misplaced. She had no idea where they were.

Gloria Sharp had not been at all enamored with Dr. Kilday in her brief encounter with him in the medical records office. Sam thought that her dislike of Dr. Kilday showed. Although he could do nothing to shake her testimony, he sensed that she was not interested in going out of her way to help him.

"Ms. Sharp, Dr. Kilday testified that the record was left unattended on your desk for a long period of time. Is that accurate?"

Gloria had not heard Dr. Kilday's testimony. She, along with all the other witnesses, had remained in a small witness room and were not allowed to hear the testimony of the other witnesses. Sam's guess that she would protect her turf was correct.

"The records were placed in a drawer in my desk. No one, other than Dr. Kilday and myself, would have known that they were in the desk. Although I do sometimes have to leave my desk, they are stored there in a safe place."

Wes then called Sue Daly, the medical technologist who had done the blood monitoring. As expected, she was an excellent witness. She appeared honest and sincere. Wes was counting on the likelihood that the jury would believe her since she had no personal stake in the disappearance of the records. Her testimony exceeded his expectations.

Sam sensed that while Gloria Sharp had not been interested in protecting Dr. Kilday, Sue Daly was more than interested in convincing the court that the testing had been done and that the Strebucin levels were within normal limits.

It was strange, Sam reflected, that two witnesses could say basically the same things, but leave lingering differences in the impressions which their testimony gave. For some reason, Sam had picked up on Gloria Sharp's skepticism regarding the missing records. Sue Daly, on the other hand, appeared very sincere. Sam had been unable to find the least crack in her testimony during depositions, and the same held true today. He even found himself wondering if Sue had more than a passing professional interest in Dr. Kilday.

The defense continued with a parade of medical experts; brief and to the point. They all expressed their opinion that Dr. Kilday had not been negligent and that the loss of hearing was simply an unfortunate consequence of Chad's illness, but one that was unavoidable.

At the end of the medical testimony, the defense attorneys rested their case. Mercifully, Judge Higgins allowed a recess. It had reached 6:30 in the evening, and the Judge wanted to allow the jury to eat. Court was to reconvene in an hour.

Sam, Ron, Anne, Alma and Lynn were eating sandwiches that Lynn had prepared at Sam's office. Sam knew that he needed to get something in his stomach but nerves would not allow him to eat much.

"We've got to decide whether we want to put on any rebuttal evidence. It just concerns me that Kilday and the defense team have apparently had the last word about Chad's hearing level. I know we put on our evidence, but I'm concerned that the jury may be left with the impression that we've tried to exaggerate."

"So what do you think we ought to do?" asked Anne. "Do you want me to take the stand, or what do you think?"

"Well, that's a possibility, although you've already testified on those things."

"Maybe it would be better if I took the stand again," Ron interrupted. "I didn't testify nearly as long as Anne and I hardly touched on those things at all. I believe I can tell them anything they want to know about how well Chad can really hear on a day to day basis."

Sam, smiling, looked at Anne. He raised an eyebrow. "Sounds good to me, is that okay with everybody else?"

Anne looked at Ron. "Sounds good to me, too."

They finished off their sandwiches, washed it all down with soda and hustled back to the courtroom. They arrived at about the same time Judge Higgins took his place on the bench.

"Anything further from either side?"

"We would like to call one rebuttal witness, Your Honor."

Higgins did not look pleased. "Make sure you keep it to rebuttal and let's keep it brief, Mr. Trestle. This case has already gone on far too long."

"We would like to recall Ron Atkins to the stand."

Sam knew he had to get to the point as quickly as possible. He had no notes and no outline of what he wanted to ask Ron. He was on his own and he knew that the defense team would jump on any mistakes.

"Mr. Atkins, you heard what Dr. Kilday and the defense witnesses said about Chad's hearing levels. Can you just tell the Court what you observe on a day to day basis with Chad?"

"Yes sir, I see him every day. I'm watching when he gets up to see what he can hear. I'm watching every chance I get because I still hope that he can hear better than what our doctors have told us. You see, I'm not watching to see how bad his hearing is, I'm watching to see how good his hearing is. I've got a son who's got to go out into the world and make it. You can't imagine what it feels like to fear that your son isn't going to be able to compete. That's true now, and that'll be true when he grows up."

"It's obvious that he's falling far behind in school. He was a good student. I don't think he's made a bit of progress since he lost his hearing. He's not able to get along with the other kids because he can't communicate with them. Used to be we had some kid over at our house every Friday night or Saturday night. But now, we haven't had anybody over in a year. He can't play on the ball team. He can't get along in Cub Scouts. He just can't get along. What I'd like to see is that he could get along. So, I'm not watching to see what he can't do, I'm praying and I'd be glad to give anything I could give if I could find out that he could hear and he could get along."

"But I had to accept the truth one day when I realized he didn't even hear a firecracker that went off six inches from his feet. Never flinched. If there was anything I could do to change that, you can be sure I'd do it, and I pray every night that things would change. But, that's just the way it is, and I'm afraid I can't change it and Anne can't change it and Dr. Kilday can't change it."

Sam had been intently focused on Ron, as had everyone else in the courtroom. Through tears in his own eyes, he saw tears beginning in

Ron's eyes. He turned and looked at Anne who was sitting at the table as if she'd seen a ghost. In fact, she had seen a Ron Atkins that she'd never seen before.

"Thank you Mr. Atkins. That will be all."

Closing arguments were anti-climactic. Although Sam had intended the closing argument to be an emotional high point of the case, he had been upstaged by Dr. Kilday. Judge Higgins, true to form, had limited each side to ten minutes in closing argument.

Judge Higgins read jury instructions and sent the jury to deliberate at approximately 8:30 p.m. Sam had no idea how long they would be in court before the jury returned. He wondered if Judge Higgins would keep them there until the jury made a decision or adjourn court and allow the jury to continue deliberations tomorrow. He hoped that it would all be over that night and suspected that he would benefit from Judge Higgins keeping the jury there until they rendered a verdict.

The time waiting for the jury was one of intense anxiety. The lawyers were helpless. Minutes dragged on like hours. There was nothing anyone could do but wait. Sam sat with Lynn and Alma. Anne and Ron were joined by Anne's mother as they sat on a bench outside the courthouse.

Anne was a jumble of nerves. She had tried to talk with Ron, Sam, and the others in the court but was unable to. She finally walked over to a corner by herself and just sat. After a while, Sam saw Wes Howell walk over and say something to her. He assumed that it had been positive since she smiled.

Sam walked down the long, dark hall leading from the courtroom, sliding his feet along the floor. He wondered how many times he had paced these halls before. How many times he'd watched Horace walk up and down the hall in the early years. What would Horace say about his performance today? Somehow, after twenty years, he still couldn't feel he'd done a good job unless he thought Horace would approve.

He bent down and got a drink of water from the ancient fountain. Air. He needed a breath of fresh air. He walked alone—he could have done it with his eyes closed—down the creaking stairs, out the front door into the cool night air. He stared up at the sky, realizing how small and minute his world was.

He looked across the front of the courthouse, down the columns, and there she stood, with her hands folded, shivering in the cold, staring at him. As he looked at her, she began walking, all the while looking at him.

And then she stopped close to him in the cold November night. He wanted to reach out and hold her but knew better.

He thought he saw a tear in her eye. Her look said it all. She had lots of responsibilities, lots of people that depended on her. Her look spoke volumes. Maybe if things had been different—times, places, people. But not now. Sam allowed himself a small smile.

"Thanks, Sam," was all she could bring herself to say.

"You're welcome, kid—anytime."

Anne turned and walked through the big doors and disappeared into the courthouse. Sam just stood and stared up at the sky. It was a big world. But in the midst of it all, perhaps there are some truths that we just know, he thought.

*   *   *

At 10:00 p.m. Sam left Alma in the courtroom and walked with Lynn to his office. He collapsed in the big chair behind his desk, sipped a soft drink from his coffee cup, and summoned Lynn to sit on his lap.

Sam sat sprawled out in the big chair in total exhaustion. Neither he nor Lynn said anything. His body ached all over from tensing the muscles in his body throughout the day. He had scarcely eaten anything and his stomach was hurting. He was feeling the beginnings of a headache creeping up his neck. Lynn gave him a kiss and rubbed the muscles in his shoulders and neck as they sat together in the big chair and waited.

At 11:00 Sam remained sprawled in his chair. He felt his face and realized that his beard looked terrible. It occurred to him that that he must look as bad as he felt. He had asked Alma to come get him when the jury came back. So far he had heard nothing, so he walked with Lynn back to the courthouse. He tried to pass the time in small talk with Ron and Anne.

The waiting group of lawyers, assistants, and family continued to wait. One by one, the witnesses who had meant to stay to hear the verdict had dwindled away. Judge Higgins was in his office, feet propped on his desk, asleep.

Sam had gone down to his office, found him asleep, and left. He knew without asking that Judge Higgins intended to stay at the courthouse until the jury came back. At 12:15 a.m., the bailiff arose from his chair near the jury room door. He opened the door and stuck his head in.

He said something, closed the door, and turned to the courtroom. "The jury has reached a verdict," he announced. The bailiff started back to Judge Higgins' office.

Judge Higgins slowly woke up, donned his robe, and made his way to the courtroom. He mounted the platform and took a seat. The bailiff led the jury into the courtroom. When everyone had taken a seat, the Judge asked, "Has the jury reached a verdict?"

Several nodded their heads and a white-haired gentlemen responded, "Yes sir, we have."

When the jury entered the room, Sam had looked expectantly at each one as they filed through the door. He had found, over the years, when the jury would look at him, that usually indicated a decision in his favor. He was unable to make eye contact with any of the jurors.

The white-haired juror glanced in Sam's direction but gave no indication of the jury's decision. Sam would have liked to have seen big smiles on the jurors' faces.

"Have you elected someone to serve as jury foreman?" queried Judge Higgins.

The jurors nodded. Judge Higgins was impatient at the late hour. "Well, who have you elected?"

"Well sir, I guess I had the questionable honor of being elected as foreman."

"And what is your name, sir?"

"My name is Jack Carter, Judge."

Sam had not wanted an older person on the jury. He felt that they tended to be more conservative in money matters and hence would probably not have been inclined to award as much damages.

Sam glanced at Ron and Anne, and neither were looking at the jury. Anne had her face in her hands. Ron had his arm around her and his head against hers.

"And what is your verdict?" asked Judge Higgins.

"We find in favor of the plaintiffs," responded Mr. Carter in a slow drawl. Mr. Carter tended to speak slowly anyway. He paused, apparently waiting to see if Judge Higgins wanted him to respond regarding damages.

The tension wanted to flow out of Sam's body, but he wouldn't allow it until he heard the amount of damages that had been awarded. Judge Higgins took foreman Carter's cue. "And do you find in favor of the Plaintiffs against all defendants or only some of the defendants?"

"Your Honor, we find that Dr. Truelove, Dr. Wilcox and the hospital are not guilty," drawled Mr. Carter, as he gave Dr. Truelove a downhome smile.

Judge Higgins adjusted his glasses from the end of his nose to their normal position. "In civil trials we don't find someone guilty or not guilty. Is it your intention to find that the Plaintiffs have not prevailed against West Side Hospital, Dr. Wilcox and Dr. Truelove?"

"Yes, Your Honor, I suppose that's what we meant to say. We don't believe they should have to pay anything to Mr. and Mrs. Atkins."

"Very well. Did you arrive at an amount of damages?"

Sam's heart was racing. He turned to look at Lynn and saw tears running down her face. Anne was sitting close to him and he could tell that she was sobbing. Anne's main desire had been to prove Dr. Kilday was wrong. She only regretted that he could not be present to hear the verdict.

Sam glanced at Wes Howell and his associates at the defense table. He saw big smiles on the faces of the attorneys who had represented the hospital and Dr. Truelove. Wes Howell looked non-committal. Sam was actually relieved that Dr. Truelove had not been found responsible.

Jack Carter seemed to be enjoying his moment in the spotlight at 1:30 in the morning in the Marion County Courthouse. "Yes, Your Honor we have set an amount of damages."

Judge Higgins also appeared to be relishing the moment. The jury could return a verdict anywhere from a minimal amount, in the event they had believed the Defendant's evidence regarding the extent of the damages, up to seven figures.

"Before you announce the amount of damages, I suppose I should make sure that I understand that you're finding Dr. Kilday as the only defendant liable for damages to the Plaintiffs, is that right?" Mr. Carter shook his head slowly. Anne continued to sob and Sam felt like screaming.

"You will have to say yes or no, so that the court reporter can pick up your answer. She can't put down anything when you just nod your head."

Sam wanted to scream.

"I'm sorry, Your Honor, that's correct. We find in favor of the Plaintiffs and against Dr. Kilday, but not against the hospital or Dr. Truelove."

"And how much have you affixed as damages?"

At this point Mr. Carter turned his gaze to Sam. "We find that Dr. Kilday should pay damages in the amount of two million dollars, Your Honor."

Sam's knees grew weak. He had never envisioned a damage award of that magnitude. He and everyone else in the courtroom were stunned. There was silence for a moment. Sam turned to Ron and Anne but words wouldn't come.

CHAPTER 43

Sam knew it would take days to get back to his work schedule. He often felt a letdown after big cases and this was the biggest he had ever been involved in. Saturday night, after a steak and potatoes supper, he was sitting in his easy chair with Lynn in his lap, reliving the details of the trial.

Sam and Lynn had taken some time to talk about what they would do with their money. They had never had to deal with a surplus of money. They had discussed building a house, buying new cars or taking a cruise. Lynn had even thought about quitting her job. They finally decided that they liked life just the way it was and that they would do with a few modifications to the old house. Sam might consider a new Jeep. Alma would get a long overdue raise.

Sam promised Lynn an extended vacation for the next summer. Lynn wondered if he would ever get around to taking her. They finally ambled off to bed and Sam got the first good night's sleep he had had in a week. He had been like a kid with a new toy. Lynn thought that Sam was more excited over his success in the case than he was over the large fee. She nuzzled next to him and drifted off to sleep.

*　　　*　　　*

On Monday morning Sam was having coffee at the Downtown Cafe when Roger Walsh, one of the older attorneys in Jasper, came in. Roger took a seat by himself, ordered breakfast, and when he caught Sam's eye, motioned for him to come over. Sam got up with his cup of coffee, walked over, and sat down across from Roger.

Roger had been one of Horace Stoneham's oldest friends. "One of my long time clients called last night, Sam. Thought you'd be interested."

Roger paused, so Sam interjected, "Who was that?"

"Jack Carter."

"What'd he have to say about the case?"

"He wanted to talk about the case. 'Course, I assured him that he did the right thing. You know Jack retired from a place over in Chattanooga a couple of years ago, but years ago he'd worked over at Evans."

Sam did not find that surprising since at one time or another just about everybody in Marion County had worked at Evans.

"He said that he had never known you, but back in the old days he had worked on the crew where your father was foreman. He said to tell you that he thought your father would be proud of you."

*   *   *

On the day after the trial, Ron and Anne for once, outslept the boys on Saturday morning. Both were exhausted. They'd decided to just hang around the house and take it easy on Saturday.

Late that afternoon, Ron had suggested that they drive to Knoxville, spend the night, and then spend Sunday in Gatlinburg. They needed some healing time, just for their family. There was plenty for the boys to do and for the first time in over a year, Anne could relax.

They got home late Sunday night. There were lots of messages on the answering machine, but Anne needed to call Karen.

"Hello."

"Hey Karen, it's me."

Karen screamed. "Where've you been? I've been dying to talk to you—Did y'all just strike it rich and disappear?"

"We just needed some time to ourselves…"

"I called Sam and he told me about the case. I can't believe it. What're y'all gonna do?"

"Gosh, I don't know. We've even talked about moving. You know, so maybe—uh—Chad could go to TSD or something. And in a way I just want to get away from here…."

"No-o-o, you can't move. I don't know what I'd do."

"It's not for sure, we're just thinking."

"How do you feel? I'd like to have seen that doctor. Doesn't it feel good?"

"I'm just numb. Of course it feels good to win the case, but somehow I'm not enjoying it like I thought I would."

"What're you talking about? This is everything you wanted."

"I know. Don't get me wrong. I'm glad we won, but more than anything, I'm just glad its over. I don't think I could stand it any longer."

"You got Doctor What's-His-Name. Wasn't that what you wanted?"

"Yeah. We got the doctor alright. But the whole thing's just—weird. It's just that it all turned out to be over some missing records. You know, we still don't really know what happened."

"Who cares?"

"I care. I'd really like to know. I don't guess we ever will. It's just bizarre. Things seem like they're never what they appear to be."

"Hey, just relax. If you don't want the money, just send it on over. When are you gonna get it? Are they gonna appeal?"

"We don't know. Sam says they can appeal, and that would delay it for a year or so. But Sam seemed to feel okay about the appeal. He says we won't have to go through the trial again for the appeal. That's all I care about at this point. I just couldn't stand to think about more legal stuff. From here on in, it's up to Sam and we shouldn't have to be involved."

"Anyway—congratulations. I'm happy for y'all."

CHAPTER 44

"After all's said and done, do you think it was worth it?" asked Sam. It was Monday evening after the trial. Ron, Anne and Sam were sitting in Sam's office doing a post-mortem on the trial.

"Hmm…It'd be hard to say," replied Anne, "I had no idea how hard it would be. It's bad enough having to go through all the expense and the depositions and the expert witnesses and missing medical records. That's one thing, but I never thought about how much trouble we were going to have in the community."

Ron had given the question a lot of thought over the last few days. "I guess that I feel like we owed it to Chad."

"During the trial, we felt so isolated," interjected Anne. "Even when I go to the grocery store it seems like people are always looking and talking. I never know whether they're talking about the lawsuit, or Chad, or what."

"One reason we wanted to talk with you," said Ron, "is—uh—we're thinking about moving. If we move to Knoxville, Chad could go to TSD as a day student for a year or two just to get his education back on the right track."

"I'm shocked," said Sam. "Never in my wildest dreams would I have thought about that."

"There are a lot of decisions to make, but, in a way, we just don't feel at home here anymore. If we're going to move, now would be the best time, since the boys are still young. Ms. McWherter feels that the sooner we could get Chad in TSD the better."

"Y'all just have to do what you think is best. But I tell you one thing, I'll never forget you guys."

"We'll never forget you, either."

"It's funny," reflected Anne, "when things are going on at the time you don't have the real picture. You know, we were worried about cancer in Chad's arm, and it turned out he lost his hearing."

Ron tilted his head, lifted an eyebrow, and looked at Sam. "Do you really know what happened to the lab results—or have a good idea?"

"I'll be honest, I just don't know. Sometimes, people just lose things. Maybe in all the hustle and bustle between departments at the hospital, or all the people looking at the medical records, it just got lost. But, if I had to guess one way or the other, I'd say Kilday probably took it."

*   *   *

Judge Higgins, used to a lifetime of long hours and hard work, stopped by the Jasper Post Office at 7:30 on Tuesday morning. On the way down the street he had seen Johnny French ducking in the Downtown Cafe.

It was fall and the mornings were getting chilly. Higgins was not looking forward to the day of office work that lay ahead. The heating and cooling system in the Courthouse had never worked well, and particularly at this time of the year, his office was either too hot or too cold.

Seeing Johnny French made him think about the Atkins case. Of course he knew how Sam had gotten the case. Sam and Johnny had been best friends all their lives. Johnny had dated one of Higgins' daughters, seriously for a while, but it hadn't worked out.

Then Sam had gone to work for Horace Stoneham, a definite negative in Higgins' book. To give Sam credit, he hadn't taken up Horace's repulsive ways, most notably the drinking, but still, anybody who'd worked for years with Horace couldn't think too highly of the Judge.

Higgins walked around the corner inside the old Post Office, walked to his box, inserted the key, and saw four or five letters in the box.

"Mornin', Judge," came a voice from the other side of the box.

"Mornin', Le Roy. You got all the mail boxed?"

"Just a minute…Yeah, I've got all yours—try to do better tomorrow."

"Thanks. See you later."

He walked over to a table and flipped through the mail. He discarded a couple of pieces of junk mail, saw several envelopes from lawyers and his eyes settled on one addressed to "Judge Higgins, Marion County Courthouse, Jasper Tennessee." It had no return address.

He opened it, took a minute to read it and then took a long, deep breath. He reached into the waste basket, retrieved the envelope, and stuck the letter back in it. Stashing the envelope in his inside coat pocket, he started for the office.

On the way to the office he thought about stopping at the Downtown Cafe. Maybe Sam was in there. He thought better of it and hurried on to his office.

*   *   *

Alma picked up the phone, answered, and then didn't bother with the intercom. "Sam—Judge Higgins on the phone."

Sam rotated around in his chair, wondering what was up. Even in the low-key atmosphere of Jasper, a call from the Judge was important.

"Sam, I'm going to need to get you and Wes Howell over here to my office. Can you be here at 10:00? That ought to give Mr. Howell or someone from his office time to get here."

"What is it Judge?"

"Just be here—okay?"

"Okay. Sure."

Sam, confused and nervous, hung up the phone. Alma walked into his office.

"What's that all about?"

"I don't have any idea. He wants us over at his office at 10:00—me and Wes Howell."

"Uh-oh."

"Yeah—uh oh."

"Didn't say what he wanted?"

"Nope, not a hint. See if you can get Anne Marie on the phone. Maybe she knows something. Oh man, please don't let there be something wrong with the Atkins case."

"Well, it's got to have something to do with the Atkins—or else he wouldn't be calling you and Wes."

"Yeah, I know. Try Anne."

Alma scurried off to her desk and Sam swiveled in his chair, slumped down and closed his eyes. "No, please don't let something be wrong…."

"Anne's on the phone."

"Hi, Anne."

"Hi Sam,—what's going on?"

"Look, you haven't heard anything about the case—or anything, have you?"

"No, don't guess so. Like what?"

"I don't know. The Judge called a few minutes ago and wants to meet with me and Wes Howell at 10:00."

"He didn't say why?"

"No—not a word. But—you—you know it's got to have something to do with the case."

"Yeah. So when are you going over there? 10:00? Call me as soon as you get back. Okay?"

*   *   *

Judge Higgins leaned back in his huge leather chair, glasses on his nose, and looked across his desk at Sam and Wes. "Don't know what to make of this, but I got this in the mail this morning." The Judge laid the letter and envelope on the table for Wes and Sam to read.

Dear Judge:

You don't know me but I know you were the Judge in Dr. Kilday's case. I know the lab reports were missing. I know because I helped take them. I am enclosing a blank one just like the form they are written on, so you will know this is for real.

I know I would be in a lot of trouble, but I want you to know. I don't feel right about it.

Dr. Kilday didn't take the reports. The lab messed up the tests, not Dr. Kilday. That's why they took the reports.

You'll never figure out who wrote this. There aren't any fingerprints on it. It's typed on a machine that you'll never find.

Wes stood up. "Well, this puts a whole new light on things—we move for a new trial. New evidence and fraud."

Sam just stared at the letter. He couldn't respond. His eyes saw white, like a huge snowstorm had blown through.

"Not so fast, Mr. Howell," said the Judge. "We don't know who sent this, you know."

"We don't have any reason to think it's false. This changes everything."

"What do you have to say, Mr. Trestle?"

Sam's first thought had been of Anne. How was he going to tell her? "I don't know, Judge, I—I'm speechless."

"Here's what we are going to do gentlemen. I'm taking note of your motion, Mr. Howell. We're going to have a hearing here in my chambers on Friday. You may discuss this with your clients, but not anyone else. Is that clear? You'd better be hitting the books in the meantime. I want briefs from both of you, in my office by Thursday. And I'll see you here first thing Friday afternoon. In the meantime, not a word to anybody but your clients—understand? I'm going to give both of you a copy of the letter, but don't let it out of sight."

Sam called Alma from a phone at the courthouse. He needed to get Anne over to the office as soon as possible. He had a legal file, one of many from the case, in his hand. He sat down and tried to get his bearings. What to tell Anne?

Who could have sent the letter? The records clerk—what was her name? Gloria Sharp. The girl from the lab? Um-m—Sue Daly. She seemed to like Kilday. Could be.

"H-m-m-m. What about Kilday? Sure. Why not? It didn't help anybody but him.

What's the Judge going to do? Don't know. If he grants a new trial, Anne will kill me.

By the time he got back to the office, Anne was waiting. She could see in an instant something was wrong. Sam looked pale.

"Come on in my office. Both of you." Alma and Anne took seats in his office and Sam laid the letter on his desk for them to read.

In a matter of seconds, tears were welling up in Anne's eyes. Alma put her arms around her. "So what does this mean?"

"Nobody knows. Wes made a motion for a new trial...."

"What!" Anne looked up, tears streaming down her face, a mixture of rage and hurt on her features. "He can't do that can he? The trial's over."

"I guess he could—but—I don't—I hope not. The Judge wants to have a hearing on Friday."

Sam and Alma tried to console Anne, largely without success, for the better part of an hour. She finally decided to take the rest of the day off, go home and call Ron.

"Boy—never thought I'd see her look so defeated."

"I know, I'll give her a call after a while, just to make sure she's alright," suggested Alma.

"Yeah. Good idea. In the meantime, I'm going to start researching...."

*   *   *

Sam worked late that night, went home, slept a few hours and was hard at work when Alma came in Wednesday morning.

"You figure anything out?"

"Not really. I'd have to say I think we're going to be okay, but I can't find any real precedents. Did you check on Anne?"

"I called last night and she still seemed really out of it. I think I'll try again this morning. I don't think she's going to work."

The phone rang. Sam picked it up and it was Wes Howell.

"What do you think the Judge is going to do?"

"Don't know for sure, but I keep telling myself he can't give you a new trial. What do you think?"

"At least we've got some hope. I just wish this had come out earlier."

"What did Dr. Kilday have to say?"

"Haven't talked to him. I really don't want to get him all worked up about it. Guess I'll have to call him this morning. He's been really depressed. I hate to get his hopes up until I know we're gonna get a new trial. Know what I mean?"

"I guess. I talked to Anne yesterday, and she's really bummed out."

Sam got a signal from Alma. "Listen, I've gotta go…talk to you later." He turned around in his chair. "What's the matter?"

"I talked to Anne. She's doing better. Said she was up all night. She thinks she's finally made peace with the whole thing. She sounded tired; but better…you know what I mean? She's going to run some errands or something and said she'd check in this afternoon."

"Good. Anne-Marie Atkins at peace with the world. That'd be a first."

CHAPTER 45

▼

"We've got to figure out what we're going to tell people happened over there in Marion County," said Edwin Fellers at the weekly partner's meeting. "I want a full written report on my desk by this afternoon Jack."

"You never told us that there was a possibility of a verdict against us, and I don't mind telling you I'm in shock. This is the first time anything like that has ever happened, and it certainly isn't going to look good. What's the story about a missing medical record?"

Jack squirmed. "I told you earlier that the blood monitoring reports were missing from the file. I never felt good about being defended by Wes Howell, but you and the rest of the firm apparently enjoy socializing with some of his partners so that's who I got. I wouldn't let Howell defend me on a parking ticket. I was humiliated. I'm going to find myself a decent lawyer and appeal."

"I agree that somebody should have told us that we had a chance of losing the case. I just thought it was a matter of course that a trial would be held and we would win."

"When I talked to Allen Gathers over at the law firm, he told me something about you walking out of the courtroom. I want to know everything about that in writing."

Kilday's countenance fell. He realized that he had been partially responsible for his demise in the Marion County courthouse. He also realized that he would be the talk of West Side Hospital for the next few weeks. Kilday was not used to dealing with failure and the impact of the jury verdict had been devastating. He knew his partners probably believed that he had taken the missing records. To combat the stress he had begun taking some tranquilizers he had prescribed for his wife.

As the meeting broke up he found it difficult to get out of his chair and walk to his office. He had a full day of appointments, but fortunately he had switched surgery schedules with another partner in anticipation of the stress from the trial.

Hunter Hollings followed Jack back to his small office. "Jack, I know that you're a good doctor and I know you didn't deserve what happened to you over there. You don't look good. If there is anything I can do to help out, I want you to let me know, okay?"

Jack appreciated the effort but was beyond consolation. He thanked Hollings and mumbled that he had to get to the hospital to make rounds. Hollings made a mental note to discuss Jack's despondency with Ed Fellers.

Jack left his office, walked back to the small break room, and got a glass of water in a styrofoam cup. If he were going to make it through the day, he knew he was going to need another tranquilizer. He washed the capsule down with a gulp of water and started for the hospital.

* * *

Anne was exhausted but decided to go to Chattanooga anyway. Still thinking about moving, she had promised to send Chad's speech records to the school for the deaf. She also wanted to talk with Maurice Washington, whom she hadn't seen since the trial. Cathy McGinnis had agreed to ride with her.

"Thanks for coming with me. With everything going on, I don't know if I could come back here by myself. At least it's nice to be going to the hospital for something other than a life and death emergency."

"I've enjoyed the ride. I'm afraid you're going to move and I'm going to miss you."

As Anne pulled in to West Side Hospital, she remembered the dreams and plans she had made for Jack Kilday. Chills ran down her spine as she pulled into one of the spaces in the huge garage. It was sunny outside, and a few rays of light filtered into the garage.

"Gosh, this is weird. I never told you about the plans I had for Dr. Kilday, did I? I had it all planned to come over here and shoot him sometime when he was leaving the hospital."

"What? No, I don't think I ever heard anything about that."

"I even came over here a couple of times and watched him leave. He parks his car right up here in the physician's parking lot."

"You're kidding. Boy, you've got a side I never saw before."

"Come on up. I'll show you where he parks."

Those plans and dreams seemed like part of another lifetime, swirling through Anne's mind. They walked up the stairwell and through the door into the physician's parking garage. Anne's eyes were immediately drawn to Jack Kilday's car sitting in the area where he typically parked.

"There's his car."

"You're kidding. Let's get out of here. I'd die if we ran into him."

"You'd die? Hurry, run over there behind that thing."

Anne's skin was crawling. She eased behind one of the huge columns which formed support for the garage. She did not want to have a face-to-face encounter with Kilday, but she could not help reliving her earlier fantasies. She stood and watched.

Another doctor drove into the garage, jumped out of his car, slammed the door, and trotted toward the doorway. He seemed to glance at Jack's car a moment and then went on.

All was quiet as Anne and Cathy stood in the shadows. Anne thought she saw some activity in Jack's car, but decided she was only imagining things. Satisfied that there were no cars coming, she edged closer to Kilday's vehicle.

"I don't know what I'd do if he came walking out here."

"Me either. Be careful."

Moving from column to column, Anne edged closer to Jack's car. She darted by the red sports car. Although she felt ridiculous, she could not help glancing in.

The chills that had earlier crept down her spine, now raced across her body. Her heart began to pound, and she ran back to the column where Cathy was waiting.

"Look here." She whispered as loud as she could to Cathy and pointed. Cathy leaned closer.

"There's somebody in there."

"Is it him?"

"I don't know—it sorta looked like him—but I was so scared, I just don't know. It doesn't look like he's moving or anything."

"Did he see you?"

"It looks like he's fallen over or something—like he's asleep."

"Good. Let's get out of here."

"No, let's wait a few minutes. What if something's wrong?"

"I'm not waiting long. Besides, what if something is wrong? What do we care? Come on."

Another vehicle entered the garage, and a white-smocked doctor got out of her vehicle and scurried toward the door. Anne and Cathy slipped back out of sight and waited.

What if she needed to do something? In a panic, she tried to consider her options. She could simply go on into the hospital, leave the situation as it was, and no one would ever know. If Kilday was in trouble, then she would have achieved the result which she had wanted for so long, and without any risk on her part.

"I'm going back over there. He still hasn't moved. Something's wrong."

"No—are you crazy?"

"I have to."

She emerged from behind the column, looked for a moment at the entrance to the hospital but found she could not pass the red sports car. She looked in the car. No movement. She reached for the door handle. Suddenly, she was back in her dream, drifting, carrying out her plans. Coolly, she realized she did not want to leave her fingerprints on the car. She remembered some napkins which she had stuffed in her purse at a fast food restaurant. Looking around, she reached into her purse, took one of the napkins and pulled the door latch.

Kilday did not move. In the passenger seat was an open medication bottle. On the console, was a cellular phone.

She grabbed the phone, closed the door and ran back to her hiding place. Cathy was speechless. Anne punched 911 on the cellular phone and heard an operator come on the line.

"Emergency Operator".

"Uh—The—there's someone passed out in a red sports car in the physician's lot at West Side Hospital."

"Who is this?"

"This is someone who's in the parking lot. I'm telling you that it looks like it's one of the doctors, and it looks like he's passed out or something."

Anne clicked off the phone, ran back to the vehicle, wiped off the phone, tossed it into the car and ran into the hospital, with Cathy close behind. She did not think she was seen.

They lost themselves, browsing in the gift shop. After a short while, Anne walked to a window where she could see the entrance to the parking garage. She saw an ambulance enter.

*   *   *

Sam was half asleep, half in thought, with books spread all over his desk. Alma buzzed, and Sam picked up the phone. "Hello. Sam Trestle speaking."

"Hello, Counselor." Sam recognized the voice of Wes Howell.

"Hello, Wes—How's everything over in the big city?" You talked to Kilday yet?"

"Actually, things are pretty interesting over here in the big city. No, wasn't able to reach him, and you're not going to believe the call I just got."

Sam's heart sank. Had they found the person who wrote the letter? "What's that?" His voice was tentative.

"One of the other doctors—Hollings—called. They found Jack in the hospital parking lot passed out in his car."

"You're kidding. Is he alright?

"Some woman found him, and called 911. Probably saved his life. Nobody knows who it was that called. They think he had a bad reaction to some tranquilizers or something like that. I think it's all going to be hushed up over here, but I thought you'd want to know."

Sam didn't know how he felt. Shocked, sad, and guilty all seemed to fit.

He hung up, and called the Atkins. No answer.

*   *   *

"Did I not understand that Anne-Marie was going to call when she got back?" It was mid-afternoon and Sam was putting the finishing touches on his brief for Judge Higgins. He needed to meet with Ron and Anne to get their feelings about which direction to take in the case. He was also anxious to relay the story about Jack Kilday's medical emergency.

"When I talked to her last night she said she'd call sometime today. I assumed we would've heard from her by now."

"Why don't you try calling their house and leaving a message on the answering machine? Or try Ron? See if they can come by sometime later this afternoon, maybe after work, so I can bring them up-to-date on everything."

Alma got Ron at work and he agreed to try to locate Anne and drop by the office that afternoon.

"Did you tell Ron about Kilday?"

"No, I knew you'd want to. I'd sure like to see the look on Anne's face when she hears that story. Didn't Wes Howell say that some woman called 911 and saved his life? I bet Anne would like to have a word or two with her, don't you?"

"Yeah or a word or two before she saved his life."

* * *

Sam heard Anne and Ron as they opened the front door and hurried out to meet them. He was all smiles. "You'll never believe the telephone call I got from Wes Howell today."

"What's that—are they going to give up trying for a new trial or something?"

"No, he said that Dr. Kilday had some kind of medical emergency this morning. Somebody found him passed out in his car. Wes said it was something about a drug reaction or something like that, but I can't help thinking maybe he'd taken an overdose."

"Did Wes say whether he was alright?" Anne asked.

"No, I haven't heard anything more. All he knew at the time was that there had been some kind of incident—apparently it was being hushed up over there. I guess you should be careful about who you tell. Anyway, I can't imagine you're too concerned about him. I figured you'd be wanting to shoot the person who saved his life."

"Oh—I think you could probably say I've gotten beyond that." Anne had a puzzling grin on her face. She looked at Ron who just grinned also.

"Sam, it's funny, I realized all this time that I had gotten so wrapped up in my own hatred that I was ruining my life, and my family, too."

"What do you mean? That's what got you and your family through this whole thing. I'm not sure you could've made it .... "

"Sam, my hatred may have carried us all the way through this thing, but then when we came to the end I realized what do we have? Did his hearing come back? Do we even know why he lost his hearing? I suppose we got revenge on Dr. Kilday, but what did that get us?"

"It got you a whole bunch of money for one thing."

"Yeah, and there's another thing. I don't feel one bit better. In fact, I felt kind of empty. Like somehow I thought getting a verdict against Dr. Kilday would make the hurt go away. Well, it didn't. Nothing changed. I was just left with this bunch of money and a big bunch of hatred. I don't want to spend the rest of my life hating somebody. I don't want my kids or my husband to spend their whole life hating people. I just don't care about the case anymore."

Sam sat and stared at Anne. At least, he thought, the case is over and decided. I'm glad she didn't come to this realization before it was over.

"I'll say one thing. This whole thing has taught me a lesson about what's important. Money or no money, I don't care what Judge Higgins does. I've learned what's important and it's not about hating people, and it's not about revenge, and it's not about getting a bunch of money from them."

Sam looked up from his file at Anne. He could tell that she meant it. "There's more to this than you're telling me, isn't there?"

Anne had that faraway grin on her face again. "I guess there's more to it than any of us know."

CHAPTER 46

It was seven o'clock on a chilly Sunday evening. Sue Daly, the laboratory technician, walked into the Lynnwood Avenue Baptist Church and took a seat near the rear. Sue was divorced, had no children, and lived alone in a house on the outskirts of Chattanooga.

After a few minutes, she looked across the small church and saw Gloria Sharp. Their eyes met and Gloria picked up her purse, walked around the back of the church to the pew where Sue was sitting. She opened her purse, gave Sue an envelope and returned to her seat without saying anything.

Sue placed the envelope in her purse, zipped it closed, and when the service began, joined in singing. About half way through the minister's message she got restless, picked up her purse, and left.

Sue got in her aging vehicle and drove home. When she got there, she went out the back door, got an armload of firewood and came back inside. It was cool and damp, and a fire would feel good.

After she got the fire going, she got a bite to eat, and sat, staring into the fire for nearly an hour. She felt sleepy as it got dark and the fire warmed her.

She dozed for a few minutes, and when she awoke, realized that she was sitting in the dark and that the fire was dying. She got up, put some more wood on the fire, walked to where she had laid her purse and removed the envelope she had received from Gloria.

"It's funny," she thought, "How you can go to the job day after day and run all those lab tests. I've been running tests for twenty years now; kinda gets to the point where you know what's supposed to come out."

At first, Sue had performed every test exactly as she had learned in school. But after a while, when her workload got heavy or she was just too tired or depressed to go on, she began filling in the figures that she knew were supposed to be there without running the tests. Deep inside, she had known that it could eventually get her in trouble, but the boredom and the depression had led her to the rationalization that no one ever paid much attention to them anyway.

She had run the Strebucin blood tests before. She knew what was supposed to go in the blanks. The doctors and nurses knew how much of the stuff to give. The tests she had run before had all been within normal limits. So, what difference could it make this time?

She had no idea that the tests would have been as critical as they were in Chad Atkins' case. But after Gloria had told her about Dr. Kilday's fit of anger in the records room, she was afraid that someone would figure it out. Obviously, she'd made a mistake. If the records were there, it wouldn't be too difficult to place the blame.

Having Gloria obtain the papers from the Atkins' file had been simple. And, in the end, Sue thought, justice had been served.

She took the missing records from Chad's file, tossed them into the fire, and watched them go up in flames. Shortly afterward, she drifted off to sleep on the couch.

CHAPTER 47

Two weeks after receiving the anonymous letter, Judge Higgins called Wes and Sam back to his office. "I've given this anonymous letter a lot of thought, gentlemen. Obviously it does throw some doubt on the case, but it can't be received as evidence since it came after the trial was over, and we don't have any way of knowing who sent it, so I've decided to overrule Mr. Howell's motion for a new trial. Personally, I suspect there's at least some basis for believing that it's true. On the other hand, one of the defendants could have simply typed it up and sent it in for their own benefit. Anyway, I don't see that there's a basis for a new trial."

Sam was elated. At the original verdict he was so stunned that he couldn't completely appreciate the moment. This time, however, he had anticipated the result. "Finally," he thought, "this thing is over." He was breathing a huge sigh of relief.

"Before you get too carried away, Mr. Trestle, we have another matter that I want to discuss. I've given the circumstances and the amount of the verdict a lot of thought. Frankly, although I think Dr. Kilday is primarily responsible, I believe the jury's verdict was to some extent a product of passion and emotion."

Sam felt his heart hammer his chest. He could feel himself beginning to panic. "Judge, whatever happened was Dr. Kilday's problem, not the jury's."

"I understand that Mr. Trestle, and frankly, I don't have a lot of sympathy. However, after a great deal of thought, I think the jury verdict is simply too high. I heard the evidence on the damages, and I've compared this with other cases of a similar nature, and I have to conclude that the jury just got carried away."

"Judge, there hasn't even been a motion to that effect."

"I understand that, Mr. Trestle, but I'm sworn to uphold the law in this county, and I can take this action on my own. I know this isn't something you're going to like, Mr. Trestle, but let me caution you not to get carried away."

Sam was fighting the urge to jump across the desk and punch the Judge. Something in the back of his mind made him realize that he needed to remain under control. His face was red, and he was sweating. He sat in his chair, fidgeting.

"Mr. Trestle, I can appreciate that we have a serious injury here, and that there is no apparent explanation for it, but I've got to do my job. Under all the circumstances, and I'm trying to be liberal here, I believe $750,000.00 would be appropriate. Of course, I can't require you or your clients to accept that. However, I do have the authority to grant a new trial, on the basis of my finding that the jury got carried away, unless you and your clients are willing to accept that figure. I'll give you ten days to make up your mind."

Sam slumped in his chair. He knew that Anne and Ron would not want to go through a new trial. He knew they were going to accept the Judge's compromise figure. He knew that, given a new trial, Dr. Kilday would not make the same mistake twice. Sam had hit bottom. He was in a trap, and he knew he had no way out.

Epilogue

Anne and Ron accepted the $750,000.00. They spent a year in Knoxville, so that Chad could attend the school for the deaf. While they were there, Ron received an offer to become personnel director for a Knoxville manufacturer. He turned it down and they moved back to the farm in Jasper. They continue to live there, working at their old jobs. Chad attends Jasper Middle School where he is a member of the school baseball team.

Jack Kilday took a three month sabbatical. Afterward, he, his wife and family moved to Atlanta where he joined a large orthopedic group.

Sue Daly left West Side Hospital shortly after writing the letter to Judge Higgins. She now works for a department store in Chattanooga.

Sam Trestle still practices law in Jasper, Tennessee.

     *   *   *